SAFE
AT
HOME

SAFE AT HOME

Sharon Robinson

SCHOLASTIC PRESS ■ NEW YORK

Copyright © 2006 by Sharon Robinson. All rights reserved. Published by Scholastic Press, an imprint of Scholastic Inc., *Publishers since 1920*. SCHOLASTIC, SCHOLASTIC PRESS, and associated logos are trademarks and/or registered trademarks of Scholastic Inc. • No part of this publication may be reproduced, stored in a retrieval system, or transmitted in any form or by any means, electronic, mechanical, photocopying, recording, or otherwise, without written permission of the publisher. For information regarding permission, write to Scholastic Inc., Attention: Permissions Department, 557 Broadway, New York, NY 10012.

ISBN-13: 978-0-439-89640-5
ISBN-10: 0-439-89640-1

12 11 10 9 8 7 6 5 4 3 2 1   7 8 9 10 11/0

Printed in the U.S.A.   40

This edition first printing, January 2007

The text type was set in 11-point Adobe Caslon Pro • Book design by Kristina Alberston

To my son, Jesse Robinson Simms,
and to the boys and girls in the
REAL Kids program at Harlem RBI
(Reviving Baseball in Inner Cities)

CHAPTER ONE

Elijah J. Breeze II, aka Jumper, shuffled his size-nine kicks along the steaming sidewalk. He was a tall boy for ten. Sweat dripped down chocolate skin and into caramel eyes. He blinked to clear the salty sting. At the corner of 136th Street, he turned left.

Seventh Avenue rocked. Black, brown, and a sprinkling of white people walked briskly in spite of the hot humid air. Cars whizzed north and south along the wide four-lane avenue. Lines of men, women, and children filed in and out of the underground subway station. A dozen or so folks stood in front of the corner grocer while several kids played hopscotch nearby.

Jumper walked up Seventh Avenue dodging leashed dogs and greeting men and women who knew his grandmother. Nervously, he fingered the coins that lined his pocket. As his fingers passed over the ridged edges, he made a mental count of his money trying to estimate how many rounds he could buy on the video machines.

He paused outside the arcade, tempted by the laughter floating out into the streets. Still, he hesitated. Every day for the past two weeks, Jumper had done the same thing: He'd walk to the arcade, stand at the door, then scurry away before someone sensed his fear. But today was going to be different. He was tired of the game he'd been playing with himself. Today, there was no turning back.

Jumper took a deep breath and stepped inside. He stood still giving his eyes time to adjust. The arcade was a little dim, but not so different from the ones he'd gone to in the suburban malls. Big fans were strategically placed throughout the room to keep it cool. Their soft hum was drowned out by bursts of electronic video games. Groups of kids clustered around the most popular games; a few loners worked the peripheral machines.

Jumper wandered aimlessly for a while, peeking over shoulders, judging the skill level of future opponents.

He recognized most of the games and knew he could defend himself against the best. He'd been playing video games for years. His father had been his most challenging opponent to date. Jumper smiled at the memory. His dad had been good.

When he came to an unoccupied machine, he claimed it. Music signaled the start of the game, and Jumper settled on the stool and slipped two quarters into the slot.

As cocky as he was with the game, Jumper wasn't sure if he wanted to display his skills yet. Still, he secretly wished one of the boys would wander over to watch him play, but there was no time to think about that. The game was loaded. Jumper grabbed the controls.

Kick! Whack! Kick! Swish! He expertly maneuvered the simulated figures. *Kick! Attack! Defend! Advance! Survival!* He made it past the first barriers and shot up his fist in triumph.

With a wide grin, he put more money into the game and began a new round. Advancing into the inner sanctum was like shooting a three-pointer from midcourt. He was invincible! *Kick! Kick! Plunge!* He destroyed his electronic enemy. *Whack! Swish!* Enemy warriors jumped into the air to avoid his mighty sword, but there was no escape.

Jumper whacked another robot, sending him flying across the dungeon floor. He laughed and fought on. He loved having control over *something*.

Sensing another's presence he looked up and met a pair of steely dark brown eyes.

"Hey," Jumper said, unnerved by the stranger's quiet approach.

"Wassup," the kid replied stepping closer.

Jumper slipped in two more quarters. This time his hands fumbled under the pressure of having an audience. But he played hard, wiping out everything in his path. Time passed too quickly. Game over.

Jumper hesitated before beginning again. "Mind if I take a round?" asked the boy watching him.

"No," Jumper answered easing off the stool. He *did* mind but knew it wasn't right to monopolize a game. Besides if he'd wanted to play alone, he could have stayed in his room.

Jumper watched as the boy reached into his pockets and came out empty. They locked eyes. *You gotta be kidding,* Jumper thought. *You interrupted my game and you don't even have the quarters?* He kept his thoughts to himself and gave the boy a "you crazy" look instead.

"Look man, let me borrow a couple of quarters till my friends come over, okay?"

Jumper didn't like the idea of loaning a stranger money. He slipped his right hand into his pocket and toyed with his remaining quarters. Even if he lent the boy money he'd still have enough left over for a couple more rounds. Jumper cornered two coins between his fingers and drew them up. Annoyed, he handed the boy the money.

The boy seemed ungrateful. He grunted words that sounded like thanks, but it was hard to tell and they certainly weren't uttered with any sincerity. "You got a name?" the boy asked as he shoved the coins into the game.

"Jumper," he answered shyly. All of a sudden the nickname he'd carried since childhood seemed too personal, too subject to ridicule in this new unfamiliar world. Would the kid laugh at him?

Sure enough, the boy snorted. "What kind of name is that?" he asked.

Jumper glared at the boy. He didn't want to explain that his dad started calling him Jumper when he was two. His parents said that he jumped more than he walked. The name had stuck with him even in school especially when he started playing basketball. But he wasn't going to share any of this with this guy. "My name," he replied stubbornly. "What's yours?"

"Marcus," the boy said. He moved his player into action.

Jumper tried to follow up with a few questions. The boy's answers were short and not exactly friendly.

"You talk funny," Marcus said. He didn't bother to look up. His eyes stayed on the screen, his hands worked the joysticks.

"So do you," Jumper shot back.

Marcus missed his next move. Jumper smirked.

Marcus missed again; this time his player was destroyed. The game ended. Marcus stood up and turned his annoyance on Jumper. "You must be new 'round here?" he grumbled.

"Sort of . . . but my grandmother's been living here in Harlem for years," Jumper said.

"So?" the boy replied. He added a couple of curse words just to show how *bad* he was.

Jumper shifted his weight from side to side. He felt edgy. Uncomfortable.

"Where you come from?" Marcus asked.

"Connecticut," Jumper replied still shifting.

"Connecticut," Marcus mimicked in a snotty voice. "Figured you were from the country by the way you dress."

Jumper checked his khaki knee-length cargo shorts with deep pockets, a turquoise short-sleeved knit shirt, and sneakers.

"Sure some funny-looking pants you got on," Marcus continued. "That's what kids wear where you come from?"

Jumper's gaze slid to Marcus who was dressed in baggy low-hanging jeans and an oversized T-shirt. He had worn the same outfit himself yesterday.

Jumper shrugged. "It's summertime," he said. "Don't you wear shorts?"

"Sometimes," Marcus answered. He looked away, pretending to be interested in some activity across the arcade.

Jumper stepped around Marcus and shot two quarters into the slot. *Whack! Swish! Attack!* Jumper quickly surpassed Marcus and advanced through the dungeon level.

Marcus stiffened and shoved his hands into his

pockets. He fumed as Jumper continued to defeat the enemy on-screen.

Jumper felt Marcus's tension and was tickled until he realized that his performance was making him a spectacle.

"Look at the boy from the 'burbs," Marcus called out to his posse across the room. The group of boys wandered over to watch Jumper. They gathered around the machine egging him on. They hurled insults, teased, and mocked Jumper in the hope of distracting him from his game.

Jumper played on, winning in spite of the pressure.

"Thinks he's a tough guy," Marcus challenged.

Jumper shoved the joystick forward and smiled as the music signaled advancement to the final level. He slipped in two more quarters determined to finish the game.

Jumper tried to focus on winning, but he was worried about Marcus and his posse. They had stopped harassing him and were now whispering amongst themselves. He wondered if they were plotting against him. He was within seconds of another win, when two of the boys broke into heavy laughter.

"Bet he can't kick butt for nothing," one of them said.

"Yeah, he'd probably jump home to his grandma," Marcus taunted. "That's why they call him Jumper."

Jumper concentrated on the screen so they wouldn't sense his fear. Suddenly, Marcus announced that it was time to move on. "It's mad hot in here," he said to his friends. "Let's bounce."

"Word," the boys replied, then pushed on.

One boy remained.

"Kelvin, let's go," Marcus called out over his shoulder.

"You go on," Kelvin yelled back. "I'll catch ya in a minute."

Jumper stood up. His game was over and he was out of money. He was taller than Kelvin by a couple of inches so maybe he could take him. He looked down at Kelvin wondering why he'd remained behind. But something in Kelvin's expression told him that he was okay.

"Sorry 'bout that," Kelvin said. "Marcus can be a rude boy, but he's really okay."

Jumper shrugged. "It's his problem."

The boy extended his hand. "Kelvin," he said smiling.

He took the boy's hand briefly. "Jumper," he replied.

"You live 'round here?" Kelvin asked.

"136th," Jumper replied. "What 'bout you?"

"Houston Projects," Kelvin said, then realized that the boy wouldn't know where they were. "They're on 103rd and First," he added.

Jumper knew exactly where that was. The summer baseball program he had signed up for was in that area. Jumper and his mother had walked past 103rd Street and First Avenue several times in preparation for his first solo trip.

"You really from the 'burbs?" Kelvin asked.

Jumper nodded. "I used to live in Connecticut," he said.

"I've never been to Connecticut," Kelvin said. "What's it like?" he asked.

Jumper took a quick mental trip through his quiet old neighborhood with its big oak trees, detached houses, and the basketball hoop on the front of his garage, then shifted to his new neighborhood with its attached brownstones, the sounds of rap, calypso, soca, gospel, and salsa filtering through the air, and kids playing toss football in the street.

Jumper looked hard at Kelvin. "Different," he answered.

"I bet. How you like living in Harlem?" Kelvin pressed

on, wondering why someone would move from any-where to live in Harlem.

Jumper hesitated. He hated Harlem. If he had friends, would he like it better? Meeting Kelvin's questioning gaze, he lied. "It's all right."

"How come you moved?" Kelvin asked.

What should he say? That his father had died sud-denly. That his mother was too sad living in Connecticut without her husband. That his grandmother had a brownstone that was too big for her and was happy to share it with her daughter and grandson.

"Long story," Jumper said curtly. He wasn't about to open up to a boy who was good friends with the likes of Marcus. "What brings you up this way?" he asked.

"Came to see Marcus."

Jumper let out a groan. "Marcus lives near here, huh?"

"Yeah."

The two boys eyed each other not sure what to say next. Kelvin broke the silence. "You ball, man?" he asked.

"Yeah," Jumper replied remembering his days on the basketball courts.

"Good," Kelvin smiled. He was glad they had something in common. "Come by the schoolyard at 136th and Eighth Avenue around four today. We be balling then," he said.

"Maybe," Jumper replied. He would love to play some basketball, but not with Marcus. "Thanks for the invite," he added with a smile.

"Okay," Kelvin replied turning away with a quick, "Catch ya later."

Jumper watched as Kelvin joined up with the other boys and left the arcade. He didn't want any other trouble so he walked through the arcade wearing his best "don't mess with me" face.

He reached the exit safely. Jumper relaxed. He felt an odd sense of victory: He'd won his first public video game, faced his first bully, and possibly made his first friend.

So, why did he still feel like this was going to be the hottest, loneliest summer of his life?

CHAPTER TWO

Jumper stepped outside the arcade and headed toward his grandmother's Laundromat. As he walked, he tried to come up with something he liked about living in Harlem. He looked up Seventh Avenue and spotted the blue-and-yellow sign in the window of Miss BB's Laundromat and had his answer. Jumper smiled. The best part was living with his grandmother.

Everyone called her Billie or Miss BB for short. Her real name was Wilhelmina Bailey. Of course, Jumper had known her for all ten years of his life, but living with his grandmother was different. Now, they spent some time together every day. It was always his favorite time of the day.

Jumper walked on thinking about his grandmother. She was so different from his mother. Well, different from the way his mother was now. His grandmother was patient, calm, fun, funny. His mom was quiet. She stayed mostly to herself and seemed far away.

Miss BB said it was because his mom was sad about his father's dying. The grief counselor had said the same thing. He understood what they meant because he felt sad and lonely, too. They both warned Jumper that it would take time for he and his mother to deal with the sadness. He had hoped that the move to Harlem would make his mom happy, but now he wondered if she'd ever be happy again.

Jumper checked his watch. He picked up his step, certain that his grandmother was aware of the time and probably already complaining that he was late. His grandmother paid him to fold clothes and make change for the customers. So far, he'd made twenty-five dollars. He was saving for a new pair of sneakers. He wasn't really worried about the time though, because as soon as he told his grandmother about the arcade and Kelvin she'd be happy to hear that he'd made an attempt at friendship.

Jumper opened the Laundromat's glass door and

wove through the crowded room past walls lined with washers and dryers. Mountains of clothes were piled everywhere. Jazz played through speakers in the corners of the room. This was his grandmother's way of infusing some joy and culture into the laundry experience. And, she repeatedly reminded him, the music helped her maintain her sanity.

Miss BB spotted her grandson and smiled. "Jumper," she called out from the doorway of her office. "You're late!" As he neared, she softened her tone. "Hurry up, boy, I need your help. Pay's good, too," she chuckled.

Jumper leaned into his grandmother and planted a loud kiss on her cheek.

"Such a charmer," she said. "Where you been?"

"The arcade," he replied, then eyed his grandmother.

"Really?" she said, looking pleased. She propped her hands on her wide hips and smiled down at Jumper. "Well? Finally got out of your room, huh?"

Jumper nodded.

"Told you there was nothing to be scared of," she said.

"I wasn't scared, Grandma," he replied.

"No. Then what was keeping you holed up in your room for the past few weeks?"

He shrugged. "Don't know."

She chuckled. "Doesn't matter. You're getting used to Harlem and that's a good thing. So, how was the arcade?"

"Pretty cool," he said.

"Now, you got to do better than that," she pressed.

"Well, they had my favorite game, so I ruled. I met a couple of kids, too."

Miss BB raised her eyebrows. She was interested. "Any of them got names?"

He shrugged. "Yeah. Kelvin was the nice one. His partner Marcus wasn't too friendly."

"Kelvin," she repeated. "Do I know him?"

"I doubt it. He's not from around here."

"Where's he from?"

"The projects."

"Which projects?"

"The ones on 103rd and First Avenue."

"Tough neighborhood," she replied. "It's near that camp you be going to tomorrow."

He nodded.

"Say he seems nice?"

Miss BB walked to the folding table and tossed Jumper a pile of clothes to fold. He moved in closer to the table, lifted a bath towel, and creased it. "Yeah. I think he felt bad because Marcus was rude," Jumper said.

Miss BB frowned. "Rude . . . how so?"

"He made a few comments about the way I dressed," Jumper said.

"And?"

"He asked to play a round so I gave up my seat and watched him for a while." Jumper didn't mention that he had loaned Marcus money. "He was good, but I was better. I guess he got mad. Anyway, he mouthed off to his buddies."

"What'd you say back to him?" asked Miss BB. It pained her to think about her grandson being teased.

Jumper groaned. He wished that he hadn't told her about the boys. "Nothing. I just kept playing my game," he replied. "Marcus moved on after a while and Kelvin stayed behind. He apologized for his friend and tried to convince me that Marcus wasn't really a bad kid. Anyway, Kelvin invited me to play basketball," Jumper added.

"Play basketball?" Miss BB repeated. "Where?" She asked suspiciously, then lit into Jumper before he could respond. "Better not be that court near the highway because if I ever catch you up there I'll whip your hide.

You hear me!" Miss BB hissed, wagging her index finger in his face.

Jumper nodded his head. He'd heard that lecture before. When he first moved to Harlem, his grandmother had told him to stay away from that playground because it was too close to the highway, and kids were known to fight there. "Not that one, Grandma. The playground in the school on 136th," he said.

"Oh, okay," Miss BB replied.

"I'm not going anyway, but I've got to find a place to play some hoops," Jumper added under his breath.

"If I hear you whine about basketball one more time," she warned. "You'll get to play plenty of basketball. You need to be reading some books this summer."

"I read, Grandma," Jumper said in defense.

"What! How you got time to read when you're always playing on that playmaker!"

Jumper cracked up. "PlayStation, Grandma," he corrected, still chuckling even though she was right. He did spend most of his time alone playing video games. Since his father died, he'd shut out everybody from his life. At first, he'd been unable to stay focused on anything: video games, school, even the chatter of close friends. But, that seemed to be changing. At least now he could concentrate on his video games. And, today he had ventured into the arcade.

His grandmother chuckled. "Okay, PlayStation," she said. "You get my point. Look, Jumper, I know this is hard for you. I hate you've had to go through so much in such a short time."

"I'm all right, Grandma."

Miss BB smiled. "I know you are, Jumper." She lifted a stack of folded clothes from the table and laid them neatly in a laundry bag, then started on another pile of clothes. "You're excited 'bout starting camp tomorrow?" she asked, looking up at her grandson.

He kept folding clothes. "Not really," he said without looking up.

"It's gonna be great. You'll see. You gotta be open to new experiences."

"But, Grandma, I don't *want* to play baseball," he reminded her.

Shaking her head, Miss BB asked, "So you say, but how come?"

Jumper avoided her questioning eyes and shrugged his shoulders. "Baseball's boring," he said.

"I don't understand," Miss BB pressed. "I thought all suburban boys loved baseball. With all that green grass and ballparks everywhere, how could they not? It's the city boys who are at a disadvantage and head to the basketball courts."

"Not true, Grandma," Jumper answered. "Some of my friends played on Little League teams, but a lot them played soccer and basketball instead of baseball."

"Okay. I guess I'm wrong, but I remember you playing some kind of baseball."

"I played some at day camp," Jumper admitted. "I stunk."

"You're such a good athlete, Jumper. I bet if you'd kept playing baseball you'd be good at it, too."

"I doubt it," he replied.

"Why you so down on yourself?" Miss BB asked.

"Grandma, I tried baseball. I couldn't hit, couldn't catch, and I was bored like crazy," Jumper said.

"So you quit?" His grandmother asked.

"No. I got hurt," Jumper replied defensively.

"Hurt?"

"Yeah. I sprained my ankle," Jumper said.

"And?"

"And, I sat on the bench, bored to tears, for three weeks until camp ended," Jumper said.

Miss BB stared at Jumper. "Something's not right," she said.

"What do you mean?"

"I don't know. Just doesn't sound right to me. What'd the doctor say?" his grandmother asked.

"Doctor?"

"Yes. You must have gone to the doctor when you hurt your ankle, didn't you?" Miss BB asked.

"Well, not exactly," Jumper said slowly. "My coach checked my ankle out and so did Mom. We wrapped a bandage around it for a while," he added.

"I see," his grandmother said. "What did your father say?"

Jumper froze. "Dad said that he didn't like quitters," he replied.

Miss BB frowned. "Did you quit or were you really hurt?"

"My ankle hurt real bad for a few days," he said.

"And then?"

"It didn't hurt as much," Jumper admitted.

"Did you take the bandage off?" his grandmother asked.

"No."

"Let me get this straight. You twisted your ankle, stopped playing ball because it hurt, and then wore the Ace bandage even when it got better?" she asked.

"That's right," he replied looking away. Jumper still remembered his father's fury.

"Is that when your father accused you of quitting?" she asked.

Jumper nodded. "He said I was using my sore ankle as an excuse."

"Were you?"

"I don't know, Grandma. What if I started running the bases and twisted it again? I could have broken it or something," he replied.

"Now you're exaggerating. What was the real reason you didn't want to play baseball, Jumper?"

He hesitated. "I told you that I was no good."

"You didn't give baseball a chance," she said.

"I did what the coach said," he replied.

"Did you practice?" his grandmother asked.

"We practiced at camp."

"I know that, but did you try practicing away from camp?"

"No. Why should I?"

"Because you've got to work harder when something

"doesn't come easily. You've got to keep at baseball until you get it right," Miss BB told him.

"You sound like Dad," Jumper grumbled. "I didn't quit, Grandma!" he insisted.

"Okay, boy. So you didn't quit," his grandmother said. She looked away from Jumper and folded a towel while she hummed.

Jumper sighed loudly. "Dad always said that you had to give a hundred percent," he said.

"Your father expected a lot," Miss BB said. "Well, I'm glad you're gonna give baseball another shot. Maybe this time you'll give that hundred percent."

"Glad somebody's happy," Jumper mumbled.

Miss BB lifted her hands in a truce. "We've been over this before. I know it's not basketball camp like you wanted, but that was already full. Besides, this is a good program. The coach at the center has a great reputation."

"The kids will laugh at me," Jumper said.

"Why's that?"

"Because I can't hit," he replied.

"Then you'll have to earn their respect," Miss BB suggested.

"How do I do that?"

"I've seen you work hard, Jumper. You didn't take to

basketball right away, either, you know," she reminded her grandson.

"I did too."

"Oh, I don't mean to say you didn't love basketball right away, but it took practice to get good at playing it, right?"

"Basketball's where the action is," he said, laughing.

"And, you like to move," Miss BB added, chuckling.

"You remember the basketball hoop I had in my room?"

"You mean the one your father got you before you were walking good?"

Jumper laughed. "Right. The one that had a big yellow spongy ball. Dad used to get on his knees and shoot baskets with me. He'd lift me up so I could dunk."

Miss BB stopped folding clothes. She turned to her grandson and gathered his face in the palms of her hands. She met his sad eyes squarely. "You must miss him something terrible," she said softly.

A stab of pain sent a jolt through Jumper's body. All he could manage was a nod.

"He worked like crazy as a stockbroker, Grandma, but never missed one of my basketball games," he said.

"Your daddy did work hard," Billie Bailey said, dropping her hands from the boy's face and turning away. She didn't want Jumper to see her tears. She walked over to one of the dryers and busied herself pulling clothes out of it. "Come on help me, boy."

Jumper pulled in by her side and emptied the dryer next to the one his grandmother was emptying. He piled the clothes into a basket and wheeled them over to the folding table. They stood side by side, working. Jumper's mind stayed on his father. "Mom used to argue with Dad all the time 'cause he got home so late," he said. "He wouldn't listen. I remember Mom telling him that the stress was going to kill him." Jumper held up a T-shirt, then let it drop to the table. He looked up at his grandmother. "It did, didn't it, Grandma?"

She met his questioning eyes and shook her head. *Maybe*, she thought. Her son-in-law was what she called a Wall Street hustler. And, from what she could tell, he did have a high-stress job especially after the stock market took a dive. She shrugged her shoulders. "I don't know, baby," she said running her fingers through his curly hair. The boy reminded her of his father — tall, skinny, brown-skinned, square-jawed, hair soft and curly.

From his momma, he'd inherited deep dimples, a pug nose, and big brown eyes.

"Did he have a bad heart, Grandma?"

Again she was at a loss. What did she know of his father's medical history? "Always looked strong and healthy to me," she finally said.

"Then, it was his working too hard. That's what killed him, didn't it, Grandma?" he pressed.

"Jumper, stop worrying about what caused your father's death. He was too young, that's for sure, but you can't measure a life just by how many years someone's with us on Earth. Got to look at what they did in those years. Your daddy loved you. And, he made *plenty* of money. He saw to it that you and your momma had everything you needed. Can't ask for much more than that." She paused then added, "Your daddy was a *good* man, Jumper, not perfect. Too ambitious for perfect. That's not bad, son . . . but it's not all good, neither."

"Next week's the anniversary," Jumper said absently.

"Anniversary?" his grandmother asked.

"Yeah. I heard Mom talking to one of her friends. She said it's been six months since Dad died."

"Oh," she replied. "Are you worried about your mother?"

Jumper nodded.

"Your mom's strong, you know."

"How would I know?" he asked.

"Just take my word for it. She is. She just needs time. So do you."

"How much time?"

"Not sure," his grandmother admitted.

"Mom hardly talks to me anymore," Jumper complained.

"I know. That will change," his grandmother reassured him. "Tell me something special you remember about your dad."

Jumper smiled. "I remember our last trip together. He said that we were going fishing. We drove all the way to Massachusetts. It was fall so the leaves had turned red, yellow, and orange. I remember wishing Mom was along so she could see how pretty the hills looked. Anyway, when we got to Massachusetts we fished some, but Dad really wanted me to see where he went to boarding school."

"Oh, yes. Mount Hermon, right?"

"Yeah. Dad stayed there for four years. I mean, he came home on holidays and over the summer, but the kids slept in dormitories," Jumper said.

"Did he like that?" Miss BB asked.

"He loved it, but I asked him if he got homesick," Jumper said.

"What'd he say?"

"Dad said he got over being away from home by joining a bunch of clubs," Jumper replied.

"Oh. Like what?"

"Dad was on the debate team, and he started an investment club. They followed the stocks in the newspaper and saved their money."

She looked impressed. "Guess your father was always thinking about making money."

"That's what he said. He liked the challenge of making money grow."

"Doesn't always grow, you know."

"Listening to Dad talk, you'd think it did," he replied thoughtfully. "Grandma, Dad started investing in stock when he was in high school. I'm going to do that, too," he said.

"Better save your money then," she suggested.

He nodded. "I am." Jumper thought about his sneakers. "Dad told me to take my time figuring out what I wanted to do when I grew up." He stopped a moment. "Said I should be able to make a good living doing what I enjoyed doing." Jumper released a deep sigh. "I asked him if he liked working on Wall Street. He told me that it had been his dream since he was a little boy. Now that I think about it, he didn't exactly say he liked his work." Jumper hesitated. "Anyway, I told him something I'd never even told Mom."

"What's that?"

"I told him that I wanted to own a basketball team. I do, Grandma. I want to own the Knicks," he said, eyes wide with ambition.

Jumper's grandmother leaned down and pecked his cheek. "Bet your dad liked hearing that, didn't he?" she said softly.

Jumper broke into a smile so big his dimples caved in. "Seemed so. He put down his fishing rod and lifted me high into the air. When I landed on my feet, he said I'd have to go to business school or law school . . . after college, I think."

Miss BB smiled lovingly at her grandson. "You can do it, Jumper," she said. "You're smart and creative. Got good genes in your body, too." She laughed.

"I guess," Jumper replied shyly. "Dad went all the way through high school and college on scholarships."

"You'll get one, too, someday."

"Well, actually Dad said that he'd set up a college fund for me with enough money in it to cover all my college expenses. He said that there should be enough to help me get started in business, too."

"I know, your momma told me about the fund," Miss BB replied. "You're a lucky boy, Jumper. Your daddy must have made a lot of money to be able to set aside some for your future. It just goes to show you how much he loved you."

"Yeah," Jumper replied. "Do you think he would want me to go to that boarding school of his, Grandma?"

"Well, did you like it?" Miss BB asked.

"It was so pretty. Sat on a hill. You could see green for miles. The kids seemed to have fun. We stayed around all weekend — yeah, I think I'd like it," Jumper admitted.

"High school's still a ways off, but I'd like to check out the school with you someday," Miss BB said.

"We could drive up like Dad and I did," he suggested.

His grandmother laughed. "I'm not so good of a driver, Jumper. I'm a city girl."

He laughed, too. "Maybe Mom will drive us," he said.

"I'm sure she'd love to," Miss BB said. "Jumper?"

"Yes, Grandma?"

"Did you catch any fish?" she asked.

"What?"

"Did you and your daddy catch any fish up there in Massachusetts?"

"Oh, yeah . . . we caught plenty," Jumper said.

They stopped talking and concentrated on their work. While he folded clothes, Jumper was lost in thought. His mother and grandmother often told him that his dad could see down from heaven. If that was true, then Jumper wondered how he felt about the move to New York City. Being a city boy, his dad had strong feelings about a kid's need for space. He had chosen the suburbs so that his son could be surrounded by grass and trees, yet he had heard his dad complain about the time he wasted by commuting. More important, if they had lived in the city instead of Connecticut, Jumper thought, they would have been closer to Madison Square Garden where the Knicks played basketball.

"Grandma, you think Dad wanted me to grow up in Connecticut?" he asked.

"Boy, you ask some hard questions," she grumbled. "A lot of people think grass and trees are best for children. But, your daddy and mom both grew up in New York City, and they turned out pretty good."

"Yeah. But what do you think? Is it better to grow up in the suburbs or the city?"

"I got mixed feelings, Jumper. The suburbs are nice and all, but the city is so full of things to do. Besides, kids are more independent here. They start riding buses and subways without their parents by the time they're your age. Some, even younger. What do you think?"

"I don't know," he admitted.

"No, I guess you don't. Once your father died, your momma didn't want to live in the suburbs anymore. I'm not sure if she ever liked living there, to tell you the truth. Maybe she should have waited a while and given you both a chance to adjust to living without your daddy, but since I was alone in my big house, we just decided not to wait. Don't you like living with me, Jumper?"

"Of course I do. It just that ... well, I miss Connecticut, too."

"I'm sure you do, boy. But just give yourself some time. In a year, you'll be settled in here. Then you can tell me how you like living in New York City."

"Jumper," Miss BB called and pointed to the still-rotating dryer. "That dryer's 'bout to stop. Pull the clothes out for me and bring them over here so we can fold them."

Jumper got the clothes from the dryer and worked alongside his grandmother for more than an hour. When they'd finished the work, he looked up at his grandmother.

"Am I done?" he asked, slapping a pile of clothes into the basket.

"Yes. Thanks for your help," she replied. "Go straight home."

Home? Home. Would he ever consider Harlem home? "Are you coming to the brownstone soon?" he asked.

She shook her head. "No. Tonight's my swing dance night," she reminded him.

"Okay," he said, his thoughts staying with the word "home." The brownstone didn't feel like home.

His grandmother read his mind. "That's right. The brownstone's home now."

"But *Grandma*," he moaned.

"*Don't* 'but grandma' me . . . best get used to it. Harlem's your home now."

CHAPTER THREE

The next morning was the first day of baseball camp. Jumper took the subway there. As he exited the station and approached the ball fields, he saw a group of boys standing outside the fence joking around. His heart sank. Marcus, the kid from the arcade, was holding court.

Jumper slowed down so he could build up his nerve. He knew that it was important not to let the boys rattle him.

Marcus looked up and spotted Jumper.

Their eyes locked.

Marcus crossed his arms over his chest and gave Jumper a menacing look. "If it ain't the boy from the 'burbs," he said to his friends. "Check him out. Thinks he better than us 'cause he once had some grass in his front yard."

Laughter rose from the group.

"And a white boy in every house 'cept his," the boy next to Marcus added.

"Slummin', aren't you?" Marcus asked.

Jumper's face burned. "Not till I saw you," he replied.

Marcus's eyebrows knitted together in a deep frown. *"My bad,"* he said.

A tall Hispanic boy stepped in Jumper's path and flashed him a friendly smile. "Hey, don't mind them. They're just jealous," he said, then introduced himself as José. The boys knocked knuckles.

"What's up?" Jumper asked.

"Say *what*?" José laughed. "Wassup with this boy's talk?"

Jumper pushed past José and ignored the other boys' comments as he headed for the ball fields. His mind raced. Marcus was trouble and was bound to heat up the harassment when he found out that Jumper couldn't play baseball. He dug the tips of his sneakers into the dirt and sent a stone flying. Of all the summer programs, why did he and Marcus have to end up in the same one!

When he reached the ball field, Jumper dropped his

backpack on the ground by the fence and slumped down next to it to watch the informal practice. He was reassured to see that some of the kids missed simple throws and grounders. But his confidence dipped when Marcus strutted onto the field like he owned it. Judging by his walk, Jumper figured that Marcus was a very good player. His suspicions were confirmed when Marcus took to the field and fired the ball to one of the boys from his group.

At eight o'clock, four coaches called the kids together. Barry Coleman, the head coach, opened the session. "Sit," he instructed.

Jumper sat, but was already planning his escape. He was definitely in the wrong place. He looked around and counted twenty-five black and Hispanic boys and girls. To help settle his nervous stomach, he made up names for the colors of skin tones around him: brown sugar, peach, coffee with cream, caramel, molasses, and cinnamon. He thought of rich fudge and caramel ice cream sundaes and stifled back a laugh.

Coach Coleman introduced himself and the other coaches, then launched into his expectations. "We'll take it slow at first, but make no mistake: Our intention is to field a team to represent Harlem at the citywide Summer Youth Fit and Friendly games."

He explained the purpose of the Fit and Friendly games, saying that they were started a year ago to encourage inner-city kids to get into shape by playing baseball. "Baseball's a good sport to teach values like teamwork," Coach said. "We'll be competitive for sure," he continued. "In fact, last year we won the championship. We might not win again this year, but we'll be prepared. Any questions so far?"

Coach fielded a couple of questions, then explained the rules. "We're here to play baseball, work well as a team, and build leaders. You're to respect each other on and off the field. Do you hear me?"

Heads nodded quickly.

"I repeat: Respect on and off the field. Am I making my point?"

Jumper glanced over at Marcus and noticed that he wasn't saying a word or acknowledging the coach in any way. He appeared not to be paying attention.

"You'll be divided into two teams, the Crawfords and the Black Stockings. The team that wins the play-offs at the end of camp will represent Harlem at the citywide games. Who can tell me where these team names came from?" Coach Coleman asked.

"They were Negro League teams," shouted a boy in the middle of the group.

"That's right. Now, I know that some of you don't have much experience with baseball," Coach said.

Certain that Coach was talking about him, Jumper looked away.

"Some of you have been playing for years," Coach continued. "Or maybe you've just watched baseball on television or gone to a game. Most of you have some knowledge of the sport or you wouldn't be here."

Jumper thought about the few Yankee games he'd seen on TV and his early attempt to play baseball. He supposed Coach was right. He knew something about the game.

"And even if you haven't played baseball, you've played some sport."

Jumper nodded along with the others. That was true. He'd played soccer for several years and basketball since he could walk.

"In time you'll learn baseball rules and gain skills. You'll have to work hard. Practice daily. Take our sessions seriously. Be on time. Ask yourself if you want to do well in baseball. Then, ask yourself why."

Coach Coleman paused and looked around at the kids. "You'll find team sports carry peer pressure. You won't want to let the team down. That fear alone can motivate you to work hard. But, just like with your schoolwork, the real motivation has to come from within. You can't work for an A in math for your teacher or your momma. You've got to want to get an A. Got to want to do your best. Got me?"

Again heads nodded, and a few murmured their agreement.

"Good attitude is what we're looking for here. I won't lie to any of you. We're asking a lot. Four weeks to field a team ready to go to a citywide game is a big order, but we'll succeed. Baseball's a tough sport. You've got to get used to failure. You'll strike out more than you'll hit. Some days you'll field well, other days you'll miss balls. It happens to the best. Kids will tease you. You may get hit with a ball or hurt yourself sliding into a base." Coach laughed. "It's a hard game that looks easy. Fools most people. But you'll all be playing and making a contribution to your team and a commitment to yourself."

Jumper listened to Coach Coleman with mounting respect. He realized that there was more at risk than making a fool out of himself on the field.

"Okay, here's how it's going to be," continued Coach. "The first week, everyone works on throwing, batting, and fielding. You'll all learn proper positioning, how to tell a fastball from a curve ball, and how to connect with the ball every now and again." He paused and looked around. "If you work hard, you'll succeed. Let's go!"

Coach Coleman and his assistant coach divided the kids into groups. Jumper stood when he heard his name called and started up to join the other members of his assigned group. His knees buckled and he caught himself before he fell. Shaken, Jumper stopped and bent down, pretending to be looking for something in his bag. When he recovered his balance, he stood back up, lifted his backpack over his shoulder, then rushed off, determined to get a grip on his nerves.

Jumper reached the far side of the field and stood beside six boys and girls. Coach told the group that in one week they'd learn to hit and field. He said that regardless of their skill level they'd be on a team within a week; week two, they'd be playing games, not sitting on the bench.

Jumper had his doubts, but decided to go with Coach's words of encouragement. He hadn't done so well with the basics of baseball before. *So what would be different this time?* he asked himself. Maybe it was like Coach said. He couldn't do it for his father or anyone else. He had to do it for himself. He had to make up for the past. He looked across the field and spotted Marcus. There was a lot at stake.

The kids spent ten minutes on the ground doing stretches before pairing up for a series of drills.

Coach Coleman took the beginners to the outfield to practice throwing and catching. They started by getting familiar with their gloves, then moved on to how to hold the ball properly. Coach lined the kids up and told them to begin with throws above the waist. Jumper was paired with a boy named Nico and realized that he was one of the boys he'd seen in the arcade. Nico was one of Marcus's posse.

Jumper pounded his fist into the borrowed glove, brought the glove to his chest, turned the palm so that it faced Nico, then flinched and lost his concentration when Nico fired the ball. The ball sped past him.

"Slow down," Jumper shouted.

"Pay attention," Nico yelled back.

They threw the ball back and forth for a few minutes. Jumper consistently missed every catch. His throwing wasn't much better: All his balls went wild.

"Can't you throw straight?" Nico yelled as he ran to retrieve the ball.

"If you'd stay in one place," Jumper shouted back.

Nico flung the ball. For once, it landed in Jumper's glove. He squeezed the glove shut and held tight just as Coach called out to the group.

"Okay, good start. The next ten minutes you'll practice throwing and catching balls below the waist. The technique is different," Coach explained. "This time you point the tips of your gloves downward like this." He demonstrated the motion, then sent the kids back to practice.

Jumper faced Nico.

"Don't they play baseball in the suburbs?" Nico asked.

"Of course," Jumper replied.

"Well, you're acting like you never played catch before."

"Just throw the ball," Jumper said as he repositioned his body. He tried to concentrate on the ball instead of his fear of it. The ball sailed toward him. Jumper reached down, snagged it, and threw it back to Nico.

"That's better," Nico called.

After playing catch for a few minutes, Jumper and Nico stopped to talk. "You're pretty cocky for a beginner," Jumper said. "You must have played baseball before."

"Street ball," Nico answered.

"Then you're not a beginner," Jumper replied.

"I never played on a real team," Nico explained. "What about you?"

"I played some a few years back. Didn't like it much," Jumper replied.

"You ready?" Nico asked.

"Fire away."

The boys parted and got into position.

Nico threw the ball. It grazed Jumper and he fell to the ground, clutching his knee.

"What are you trying to do?!" he yelled.

"Sorry," Nico called back. "You okay?"

Jumper slowly got to his feet. "Yeah. I guess so," he said.

Jumper was determined not to let Nico get him

down. He retrieved the ball, repositioned himself, and threw to Nico.

Nico caught the ball and fired off another wild ball to Jumper. The throw was high.

Jumper turned his glove up and reached up for the ball. He missed it. "Why don't you try to throw a decent ball?" Jumper shouted angrily.

Nico laughed. "Let me try again. Let's see if you can catch this one." Nico looped a slow pitch that landed below the waist and right into Jumper's glove. "Is that better?" he yelled back.

Jumper ignored him and fired a ball back to Nico. He had a strong arm if he could just control it. The boys threw a few more balls back and forth. Jumper was relieved when Coach called them together and taught them how to catch fly balls.

Jumper trotted to the outfield to practice. He ran past balls, tripped over his feet, and was blinded by the sun. By midmorning, Jumper was ready to toss in his glove.

The next rotation, batting wasn't much better. Jumper stepped onto the plate, mentally reciting the steps Coach had demonstrated: elbows up, bat back, eyes on the ball, full swing. He bent his knees and pointed his left toe inward. He kept his eye on the ball and swung.

Missed!

No matter how many times Jumper swung his bat, the only thing he connected with was air.

Lunch came just in time. One more swing and a miss and Jumper would have screamed. He filed after the others into the lunch line. When his tray was full, Jumper headed into the lunchroom and nearly bumped into Kelvin.

"How's it goin'?" Kelvin asked.

"Going," Jumper replied.

"Not like basketball, huh?"

"Got that right," Jumper replied.

"Well, good luck," Kelvin said and kept going.

Jumper put his tray down at an empty table, his eyes followed Kelvin to a table with Marcus. Jumper had barely bitten into the dry, lukewarm burger when two girls dropped their trays at his table.

"Mind if we sit here?" the taller of the two girls asked. Without waiting for a reply, she and her girlfriend eased onto the bench across from him. "I'm Sabrina and she's Nia," the girl said, pointing to a short, brown-skinned girl with two braids that hung over her shoulders.

Jumper nodded toward the girls. "Jumper," he said, then took another bite of his burger.

"Jumper? Interesting," Sabrina said dismissively, then continued her conversation with Nia.

"I *tried* to make friends with her," Sabrina said.

Nia gulped down a chunk of hot dog and added, "She moved onto my block!"

"She's a nerd. Says things like, 'totally, and, it's very hot outside . . .' Bet she always answers questions in class, too."

Nia cracked up. "Problem is, even *more* white people gonna move from downtown into Harlem," she said.

"Yeah. My mom says they're gonna raise our rent for sure," Sabrina said.

Nia groaned. "Where we gonna go when that happens? As it is, Harlem's the only place in Manhattan we can afford. We'll be pushed into the Bronx soon," she said, sinking her head in her hands.

Jumper was hooked by their story. Was there a white girl at camp? He looked around thinking he'd missed her in his quick assessment of the campers.

Sabrina leaned within an inch of Nia's face. *"You been in her house?"* she whispered.

"You better believe it!" Nia replied.

Sabrina's large brown eyes lit up. She slapped Nia on her arm. *"Say what?"*

"That's right," Nia said proudly.

"Bet she got mad stuff up in her room?" Sabrina suggested.

Nia filled her in. "Got more toys, video games, and stuff than a toy store."

"You steal anything?"

"Sabrina!"

Jumper's mouth fell open.

Sabrina straightened her body. "Well," she said looking from Nia to Jumper defensively. "If the girl's got too much stuff, she wouldn't miss a few small things. You better not catch me up in there. I'd take something," she said, then faced Jumper and added, "What you looking all shocked about?"

Jumper closed his mouth. "You think that just 'cause someone's got a few more things than you, it's okay to steal?"

"She didn't mean it," Nia said, glaring at Sabrina. *"Did you, Sabrina?"*

Sabrina shot Nia an evil look. "Guess not," she said. "Just not sure I like all the changes, that's all."

"Uh . . . change isn't all bad," Jumper said, thinking of a conversation he'd had with his grandmother.

"Truth is," Nia agreed, "when a brownstone gets fixed up, it makes my block look better and makes me proud to live here."

"Yeah," Sabrina said in agreement.

Jumper asked Nia and Sabrina to point the girl out they were talking about.

"What's her name?" he asked.

"Dakota Fisher," Nia said.

"Can you imagine being named after a state?" Sabrina asked.

"White people can be so weird," Nia answered. "But she can play some ball."

Jumper slumped. So, even a girl named Dakota could play baseball.

"Yeah. She's one of the best pitchers I've seen," Sabrina said. She looked boldly at Jumper. "You got some nice dimples," she said.

"Nice curly hair, too," Nia added.

Jumper's cheeks blazed with embarrassment.

"Where you from?" Sabrina asked.

"136th Street," Jumper replied, happy they'd gotten away from talking about his looks.

"Really?" Nia said. "Between what avenues?" she asked.

"Seventh and Eighth."

"So, we're neighbors," Nia chirped. "I live on 146th and Convent."

Sabrina stared at Jumper over her hot dog. "When'd you move to Harlem?"

Jumper shifted uncomfortably on the hard plastic bench. "A few weeks ago, after school finished," he said.

"Moved?" Nia repeated, a bit annoyed that her friend had picked that up first. "From where?"

"Connecticut," Jumper replied.

Sabrina brightened. "I have a friend from Connecticut. I met her at sleepover camp last summer. She's a white girl."

"Not everybody from Connecticut's white," Nia snapped.

"I know that," Sabrina barked.

Nia cocked her head to the side and glared at Sabrina. "Give it a rest," she ordered.

Sabrina backed off. She turned her attention to Jumper. "So, what position do you play?"

"Position?" he asked, confused by the quick shift in conversation.

"*Baseball,*" Sabrina replied. "*Remember? That's why we're here!*"

"*Oh,*" Jumper groaned. For a few happy moments he'd forgotten all about playing. He pushed his tray away. "I'm not sure," he replied.

"What position do you usually play?" Nia asked.

"I don't."

"Don't what?" Nia questioned.

"Don't usually play baseball," he admitted.

Sabrina frowned. "Then *why'd* you come to a baseball camp?"

"Good question," Jumper replied gloomily.

"You heard Coach," Nia started. "He said that he's gonna field a team made up of those with and without baseball experience. Jumper will be all right."

"Um," Sabrina mumbled, unconvinced. "*I guess.*"

"We've been playing baseball and softball for a couple of years," Nia told him.

"Well, I've been playing basketball for years," Jumper replied.

"I like basketball, too," Nia said.

Now he was surprised. Nia seemed too short to play b-ball.

"How do you like baseball so far?" Sabrina asked.

"It's just my first practice," he reminded her.

"That's true. Don't worry, it'll get better when we start playing actual games."

"I can't wait," Jumper said sarcastically.

"I wonder which team you'll be on?" Sabrina questioned. "Hope it's not the Crawfords," she added.

"Why's that?" Jumper asked.

"Oh," Nia replied, looking worried. "Because Marcus is the captain, and he doesn't have much patience for beginners!"

"Or the new kid on the block," Jumper added.

"I take it you've met Marcus, huh?" Nia asked.

Jumper lifted his head. "Unfortunately."

"Oh, come on . . . he's *not* so bad. Is he, Nia?" Sabrina winked at her friend.

"He's a jerk!" Jumper snapped.

"Well . . . um . . . he sometimes acts worse than he is," Sabrina said, looking over at Nia.

"Yeah," Nia agreed. "And don't mess with his sister."

CHAPTER FOUR

Jumper arrived home, whipped and frustrated. He was certain that baseball camp was a major mistake. All he had to do was convince his mother of this fact. He was willing to work all day at the Laundromat or help his mother unpack boxes, or even clean the brownstone just as long as he didn't have to battle that little white ball.

He unlocked the massive carved mahogany doors, swung them open with one hand, and shouted from the open doorway, "Mom!" He waited for a reply. Nothing. He called out again, then he slammed the door, dropped his keys on the table in the foyer, and raced up the steps calling for his mother.

"Jumper. Stop yelling," Carolyn Bailey Breeze shouted from the top floor. "I'm in my room."

He took two steps at a time, raced past his bedroom and up the last stairs, and landed noisily on the top floor. His eyes widened. Boxes, some empty, some still taped, covered every inch of the hardwood floor. His mother was buried in the middle, lost in chaos and clutter.

"Mom?" he called softly. His baseball troubles faded with the sudden concern he felt for his mother.

Carolyn didn't look up. "I just got a call for an art teacher's job. I start work next week. These boxes have to go," she said, tossing the contents of her box to the floor.

Jumper stared at his mother. "You got a job?" he repeated.

"Uh-huh," she uttered, still more preoccupied with the contents of a box than with him.

"Oh," he said. "Where?"

"I'll be teaching art in the new high school on 135th Street," she replied.

"But, it's the middle of July," Jumper said, disappointed. His plan to quit camp would backfire if his mom went back to work. She would never let him stay home alone.

Carolyn glanced up at her son quickly, then went back to pulling more stuff out of the box.

He heard her sigh.

"They're bringing the new teachers in a few weeks early so they can get ready for the start of school," his mother reported.

Jumper sank to the floor, pushing the clutter away. He sat cross-legged, resting his elbows on his knees. His body slumped forward, his chin supported by fisted hands. He studied his mother.

She seemed to have gone from depressed to manic while he was at camp. She hadn't even asked him about his first day.

Jumper opened the lid of the box next to him and peeked inside.

His mom looked up. "I saved that box for you," she said. Her voice sounded calmer now. "Oh, Jumper, I'm sorry . . . I forgot to ask about your first day at camp. How did it go?"

He met her eyes and saw a deep sadness that matched his own. "It was okay," he answered.

"Just okay?"

"Yeah . . . well, it was only my first day."

"I know, but did you meet any kids?"

He shrugged. "A couple of girls ate lunch with me."

"How was the baseball part?"

"Miserable," he replied.

"Why's that?"

"I stunk, that's why."

"Jumper, you said yourself that it was just the first day."

"I wish it was my last."

"Four weeks, Jumper. We agreed."

Jumper glared angrily at his mother. All of a sudden, he was boiling. He wished he could slam his fist into a punching bag or scream until his lungs wore out or just tell his mother that his life was broken. The beat was wrong. And baseball camp wasn't the answer.

"I didn't agree. I was forced," he shouted.

Carolyn stared at Jumper and allowed the sting of his words to sink in. She couldn't blame him.

"Just give it a chance," she suggested.

"I went today, didn't I?"

"It's best, Jumper," his mom said.

He looked up, eyes full of emotion. "So you and Grandma say."

"You need to be around other kids."

"If we hadn't moved, I would have been around kids I knew and liked," he reminded her.

"We had to move, Jumper," she said sadly.

"Why did we *have* to move?" he persisted.

"Because we needed to be near family. Well, I did. And I figured since we're starting over anyway, we might as well go back to our roots," his mother added.

"*Your* roots," Jumper said coolly.

"I hope they'll become your roots, too," his mother said softly. "I think you'll learn to like living in the city."

Jumper stared at his mom. They'd been over this all a million times before.

"I don't want to go back to camp," he finally said.

"You can't quit, Jumper."

He glared angrily at his mother. "Why not?" he asked.

"Because quitting isn't always the right choice. Sometimes you need to work through things that are difficult."

Jumper stood and paced between boxes. "I wanted to go away to sleepover camp with my friends! Why didn't you let me?"

His mom hesitated. "I couldn't send you away this summer," she said. "I needed you around. It was just too hard . . . what with your father being gone and all."

Jumper shrugged his shoulders. "What difference does that make?"

"What do you mean?" his mother asked.

"You haven't talked with me in months," Jumper replied. "All you do is tell me what to do. You told me that you're selling the house. Now you've told me that you're going back to work. You told me that we're moving to Harlem. I should have gone away to camp and just let *you* move," he added stubbornly.

His mother covered her face with her hands and sobbed. Jumper looked on uncomfortably. He hadn't meant to make her cry.

"I guess moving so soon after your father's death wasn't such a good idea, but I couldn't go on living in Connecticut without him. It was just too hard for me. Can you understand that, Jumper?" his mother said quietly.

He nodded toward his mother.

"I knew my mother would help us both heal. Our life with your father will always be a part of us. Someday, the memories of those years will make us laugh and cry. We'll be able to look at family photographs without hurting."

"I'm okay, Mom. Really," he whispered.

"I know you are, Jumper. So am I," she said. "Come to me," she offered and held out her arms.

He crossed the room and leaned into his mother's embrace. They hugged.

"Sit with me a few minutes," his mother suggested.

"Okay," he agreed.

They sat together on the floor.

"Your grandmother called. Wanted to know if you'd gotten home yet," Carolyn said.

Jumper glanced up smiling. "Is she coming home for dinner?"

Carolyn laughed. "No. She's going dancing at the Savoy tonight."

"Again?" he asked.

Carolyn smiled. She wondered if her mother had a boyfriend. It was the second night in a row that she'd missed dinner. Or maybe she was just giving them a chance to work out their problems without leaning on her. "Swing dancing," she said with a laugh, wishing she'd inherited such a free spirit.

"Think Grandma has a boyfriend?" Jumper asked.

She laughed out loud. "I don't know," she replied.

"Think you'll ever get married again, Mom?" Jumper asked.

She shrugged. "Who knows? Right now I want to get us straight."

"Remember the counselor said it would take a year or more."

His mom nodded. "Yeah. A year won't be long enough. We loved him so . . . didn't we?"

"Dad loved us, too, Mom."

"That he did. And he'd want you to kick butt at camp, you know."

"I guess," Jumper replied, thinking back to his argument with his father when he'd quit baseball the last time. "Thing that gets me is that Dad hated baseball."

"Your father didn't hate baseball, Jumper. He played baseball all the way through high school. He told you about that, didn't he?" his mother asked.

"Yeah, but he didn't watch it on TV or go to any games," he reminded his mother.

"I think he lost interest in baseball after high school. Your father was more concerned about making the dean's list than he was about sports," Carolyn said. "But guess what I found today?"

He shrugged his shoulders.

"Look in that box over there. The one I said was yours," she said, pointing to the box he'd opened earlier.

Jumper stood and moved over to the cleared spot next to the box. He peered in. His father's high school yearbook was on top. He pulled it out and flipped through the pages. He found his father's graduation photo and laughed. His dad looked so different from how he remembered him. He read the inscriptions. "A risk taker." "Charmer." "Destined to be rich."

Jumper put the yearbook down. He looked over at his mother. She was digging through a box filled with art supplies. It'd been a long time since he'd seen her paint.

He dug deeper into the box and found a fountain pen that belonged to his dad, a silver chain-link bracelet with his father's initial carved on a plate, and a photo album. Jumper stopped to check out the photos. They were all of his dad's high school baseball team. Many of them included a shot of his high school baseball coach with the team. Mixed in were photos of his dad's friends and even a couple of pictures of girls. The last shot was of his father standing next to his beloved first car.

Jumper closed the album and set it aside. He picked up the bracelet and tried it on. It was too big. The heavy metal chain slipped off as soon as he dropped his hand. He set it next to the album.

At the very bottom of the box, Jumper found a stiff, battered, leather baseball glove. He plied it with his fingers breaking down some of the stiffness. He slipped it onto his left hand. It fit perfectly. He fisted the glove molding it to his hands.

Jumper smelled the glove, searching for traces of his father's scent. He fought off tears. Without lifting his eyes, he spoke to his mother. "He kept his glove?"

"Yeah. Just goes to show you that he used to like baseball," Carolyn said. "I think it was the only sport your dad played in high school. When he was a senior, the team won state championships, you know."

Jumper shook his head. "Yeah, I remember," he said, then turned his attention back to his father's glove. It was stiff, but if he rubbed it with oil it would soften up.

"I'll take this," he said to his mother and put the rest of the things back into the box. "Keep the other stuff. Someday, the bracelet will fit me."

His eyes rose to meet his mother's. She was smiling at him. He wanted to tell her that she didn't need to worry about him, but he could see that wasn't necessary. In that split second, she knew.

CHAPTER FIVE

On the fourth day of camp, Coach Coleman pulled Jumper aside and told him to meet him at the batting cage after lunch.

Embarrassed by being singled out, he opted for a protein bar from his backpack instead of going to the cafeteria.

"I didn't see you in the cafeteria," Coach said as soon as he arrived at the batting cages.

"Didn't go," Jumper replied, pulling himself to a standing position.

"Why?"

"Wasn't hungry."

"It's hot out here and you're working your body hard. You need to eat. Don't miss lunch again."

Jumper got the point but he still defended his decision. "I didn't miss lunch altogether," he replied. "I ate a protein bar, that's all."

"That's a snack," Coach reminded him. "Now, let's get some extra practice in."

Jumper stayed at the batting cages until Coach Coleman dismissed him. He quickly gathered up the balls and put them back in the machine. Coach waited on the other side of the fence.

"You looked good in there, Jumper," Coach said as they crossed the grass. "How did it feel to connect with the ball?"

"Powerful," Jumper replied cheerfully.

Coach smiled. "Like Barry Bonds?"

Jumper laughed. "I guess."

"You're catching on," Coach said. "Stick with it."

Jumper nodded. "What if I can't hit the ball when it's pitched to me?"

"You'll hit it. Not every time, but eventually you'll hit it."

"I don't get it, Coach. Why is it easier to hit the ball when it's pitched from a machine?"

Coach laughed. "Less pressure, more precision," he explained. They stood and talked for a while. Jumper learned about the hitting zone and how to pivot his body so that he'd increase his chances of hitting the ball. Coach talked about the need to wait as long as you can before shifting your body into the hitting position. "You can't rush the ball, Jumper. Let the ball get to you, keep your head down and your eye on the ball. This afternoon I want you to practice following the ball from the pitcher's hand to the catcher's mitt."

Jumper nodded.

"The only way to get better is to practice, practice, and keep practicing. Got it?"

"Yes, Coach."

"Now, go back to the field and spend the rest of day hitting, then meet me in my office after camp lets out."

Jumper worked hard for the remainder of the day. After the others left, he headed over to the coach's office.

Coach Coleman was watching a Yankees game when Jumper came in. "You like the Yankees?" he asked.

"Yeah. I guess," Jumper said, taking a seat across from coach.

"Got a favorite player?"

"Jeter."

"Why Jeter?"

"He's smooth."

"Smooth?"

Jumper laughed. "Yeah. You know the way he lifts his body into the air, catches a fly ball, completes a double play."

"Elegant almost," Coach Coleman said as he nodded in agreement. "You want to play shortstop?"

Jumper shook his head. "Not me, Coach."

"Why's that?"

"I can't catch," he admitted.

"Can't?"

"Well, not very good."

"*Well,* Jumper. Not very *well.*"

"Well," he repeated.

"Do you expect to be catching balls like Derek Jeter after a week?"

"Maybe not like Derek, but certainly better than I'm doing. You think it's the glove, sir?"

"What do you mean?"

"Do you think the glove's too big?"

"Let me see it."

Jumper passed his glove over to Coach and waited.

"Where did you get this glove?" he asked.

"It was my dad's."

"When did he play?"

"In high school. His team won the state champion-ships. Dad used to brag 'bout how good he was. Could have played in college, but didn't. Mom thinks he was more interested in getting A's than in sports. Anyway, Mom gave me a box filled with things my dad kept from high school. I think she hoped that I'd like baseball better if I used my dad's old glove."

"Really? Well, your dad must be glad you're learn-ing the sport."

He hesitated. "He's dead."

"Oh," Coach said. "I'm sorry. I didn't know. That makes the glove even more special. You should treasure this," he said, turning the glove over in his hands. Coach Coleman handed the glove back to Jumper. "When did your father die?" he asked.

"Six months ago."

"I'm sorry, Jumper. Well, I can tell you that your father would be real proud of you."

"Really? Why's that?"

"Because you're trying so hard. Jumper," Coach began.

"Yes, Coach."

"Next week I'll be dividing the campers into teams.

I've decided to put you on the Crawfords. Marcus Johnson is the captain. Do you know him?"

His heart fell. "We've met," he said dryly.

"Got some problem with him?"

"Um . . . Not really, Coach."

"Okay. Good. Marcus can be tough on new kids, but will come around as he gets to know you. Anyway, I want to work with you on your skills after camp. If that's okay?"

"It's fine, Coach."

"Then let your mother know that you'll be coming home late for the next week." Coach glanced over at his clock. "Now, get on home before your mother starts to worry. See you tomorrow, Jumper. We'll start with throwing and catching."

"Right, Coach."

That was it. Jumper tossed his backpack over his shoulder and walked out of the front door, and almost bumped into Nia, Kelvin, and Dakota.

"Hey," he said.

"We waited for you," Nia said.

"Really? Why?"

Nia shrugged. "We live near you," she suggested.

He cast a doubtful look at Nia and then turned to

Kelvin. He and Kelvin had barely spoken more than a few words to each other since camp began. And Kelvin *didn't* live near him.

"Well, I saw Coach speak to you. What did he want?" Kelvin asked.

"Not much," Jumper replied.

Dakota jumped in. "Didn't he say anything?"

"He asked me if I like the Yankees," Jumper said, "and who my favorite Yankee player was and why."

"Coach is slick like that," Kelvin said. "He found something out about you and you didn't even know it."

"He did the same thing to me," Dakota said. "Asked me all these weird questions about pitching. The next day, he started training me to be a pitcher. Now, I love it," Dakota said.

"He offered to help me after camp," Jumper added, feeling more comfortable knowing that Coach had pulled Dakota aside, too.

"Did he tell you which team you're on?" Kelvin asked.

"Crawfords," Jumper answered.

"You know Marcus is the captain," Kelvin said.

"I know."

"Come on. Let's walk home," Nia suggested. "That

way we can leave Kelvin at his building and stop and get some ices. You do like ices, don't you?" she asked Jumper.

"Uh-huh, but that's a long walk," he said thinking of his aching muscles.

"Oh, come on," Dakota said pulling on his sleeve. "We do it all the time."

Kelvin looked around. "Actually, I've got plans. I'll see you tomorrow," he said and took off on his own.

Jumper wasn't surprised that Kelvin didn't want to be seen with him. Still, he appreciated his hanging around to find out what Coach wanted. He tossed his backpack over his shoulders and pressed on with Nia and Dakota. They laughed and talked as they walked. He liked both girls. They were having so much fun that Jumper hardly noticed the distance. At 125th and Seventh, they stopped for mango ices and sat on the sidewalk in front of the store to eat them.

"Jumper," Nia said.

"Yeah."

"I should have told you before, but Marcus is my brother," Nia told him.

Jumper shook his head. "I had no idea," he said.

"It doesn't matter," Nia offered.

"Except that he's been messing with me since the first time we met. What's he going to say about you hanging out with me?"

"It's none of his business!" Nia stated firmly.

"He won't bother Nia," Dakota added.

"Really? I didn't think bullies cared about anyone," Jumper suggested.

"That's where you're wrong," Dakota replied.

"Wrong, how?"

"Marcus pretends to be a bully, but he's really not. I've never seen him actually fight anyone. He's just mouthy like I told you the first time. He'll be all right after he gets to know you," Dakota said.

"So everyone says, but he hasn't said one word to me in a couple of days. He just gives me this angry look," Jumper replied.

"I know how he can be," Dakota continued. "He was tough with me until he saw me pitch, then he lightened up."

"That's where you've got an advantage over me. I'm not good at baseball," Jumper explained. "He'll never like me."

"You'll get better. Besides, Coach is gonna work with you. He won't let you down," Dakota assured him.

"I'll help you, too," Nia offered.

"So will I," Dakota chimed in.

"We can stay after camp and practice with you," Nia suggested.

Jumper smiled. "Okay."

Dakota looked at her watch. "I've got to get on home and walk my dog," she said.

Nia groaned. "She's got this funny-looking black dog with ratty hair," she told Jumper.

"She's a puli with dreadlocks and a million names."

"A million names, huh?" Jumper repeated.

"Yeah. We waited a long time for the dog, so my sister and I just kept coming up with new names. We call her Tallulah. Want to hear her whole name?"

Jumper laughed. "Can't wait," he said.

"It's Queenie, Tallulah, Tigi, Wave, Pasta, Rasta, Shamrock, Homer, Oakie Fisher."

Jumper and Nia looked at Dakota like she was crazy.

"Leave it to a white girl," Nia said laughing. "If we had a dog, he'd be called Dog — or Brownie, if he was brown."

"*Well,*" Dakota said defensively, "we love our dog. She's a member of our family."

"I'll bet she *is*. Does she have her own room, too?" Nia asked, chuckling.

"No, she sleeps with either Meredith or me."

"I had a dog once," Jumper said to break the building tension.

"And, what was *its* name?" Nia questioned.

"Cole."

"That's a cute name. What kind of dog was he?" Dakota asked.

"A golden retriever."

"What happened to him?" Nia wanted to know.

"He ran away."

"Really? Did you put up signs?" Dakota asked.

"It was the day the moving truck came to our house. I don't think he wanted to move to New York," Jumper said.

"Like dogs have feelings," Nia said in disgust.

"They do!" Jumper and Dakota said in unison.

"All right," Nia said. "I'm sorry."

"Why are you always down on things?" Dakota asked.

"Maybe I got reason to be," Nia retorted. "I didn't grow up in Connecticut or the Upper West Side like you two. My father never allowed us to have a dog, a cat, a turtle, or even any privacy. So forgive me if I can't share your concern for a dog!" She jumped up, brushed off her shorts, and looked down at Jumper and Dakota as if to say "What's your problem?"

Jumper and Dakota followed Nia's lead in silence. Jumper wanted to ask Nia more about her father. He sounded mean. Maybe that was why Marcus was hard on everyone.

"Where's Sabrina?" he asked after they'd been walking in silence for a while.

"Sabrina's got to pick up her baby brother by three-thirty, so she cuts out of camp as soon as it's over," Nia said.

"Oh, I didn't know she had a little brother," Dakota said.

"Tommy's two," Nia replied. "He's so cute!"

"My mother wouldn't let me pick up my sister at day care until she was five," Dakota said.

"Well, your mother probably had money to hire a nanny?" Nia replied.

Dakota nodded. "True."

Jumper walked ahead of the girls. Let them bicker about someone else's life. He wanted no part of it. Girls were such a trip!

"Hey, Jumper, wait up," Nia shouted and raced to catch up with him. "What do you think this is? In Harlem, women don't walk ten steps behind the man; they either walk with them or in front of them," she said with a laugh.

Dakota was keeping pace now, too.

Jumper stopped in front of the arcade. "I'm going inside. I'll see you two tomorrow," he said.

"Can't we go in with you?" Nia asked.

"Only if you promise not to talk," he warned them. He'd had enough of silly girl talk.

The girls followed Jumper into the arcade and cheered him on while he played a couple of games. They took turns playing several simulated games of baseball. Nia and Dakota laughed as Jumper pretended he was a baseball star. Jumper didn't care. For those brief moments, he was a star.

CHAPTER SIX

The next week, Jumper stayed after camp each day for extra practice. He spent hours playing baseball video games and watching baseball games on TV. He even went with Dakota and her father to a Yankees game where he learned how to score a game and call the plays. By the end of the second week in camp, Jumper was more confident and had to admit that he was starting to enjoy playing. He decided that what baseball lacked in action it made up for in strategy.

By the third week of camp, Jumper was nervous but excited when Coach announced that the practice games were over and the real games between the Crawfords and the Black Stockings would begin.

The transition from practice to team games was hard. Under the pressure of play, Jumper forgot the skills he had learned. He fell into a slump. He sat on the bench, fiddled with his glove, and watched the game with mounting anxiety. Soon he'd have to stand in the batter's box and prove himself. And there was only one way to do that: Hit the ball.

By the top of the ninth inning, the Black Stockings led 4 to 1. The Crawfords were at bat.

José stepped to the plate. He was a solid base hitter and a very fast runner. Jumper had studied him during their practice games. José usually got on base and often stole at least once during every game.

Jumper watched as José bent low, kept his head down, and held his bat away from his body. It looked like he planned to bunt. The pitcher sent the ball straight down the line. José swung full, driving the ball deep into the outfield where it landed behind a flustered Nia. One of her teammates raced over from center field, scooped up the ball, and tossed it to Sabrina at first base just as José's cleats touched the bag.

Safe! The Crawfords jumped off the bench and cheered.

Now Dakota stepped from the on-deck circle into

the batter's box. She couldn't hit, but no one hassled her because she was such a good pitcher.

"Strike one!" the umpire shouted at the first pitch.

Dakota readied again. A fastball whipped past her body just above her waist. She took a chance.

"Strike two!"

Dakota looked around nervously and caught Jumper's eye. He sent her an encouraging smile. She faced the pitcher and waited. As the ball neared her body, she pivoted and overswung. Her body twisted like a top.

"Strike three!"

With one out, Danny, a confident, tall, skinny boy from the South Bronx, stepped up. He had a strong arm. He could throw long and hit hard. As predicted, Danny whacked the ball into center field for a solid single. José landed safely on second.

Aisha was up next. Jumper liked her. She was quiet with a kind smile. Aisha hit a perfect sacrifice bunt as she'd been instructed to do. She ran, but was tapped out by the pitcher. The play worked. Danny advanced to second and José made it to third.

The Crawfords were hot!

Marcus strutted confidently to home plate. He readied his bat.

José bent down low and nodded toward Marcus. José was determined to make it home. All he needed was for Marcus to hit a single and he was gone!

The pitcher wound up and fired a curve ball. Marcus swung hard and missed. He held tight with the second pitch. The umpire agreed. "Ball One," he shouted. Marcus bent his lean body, curved his toes inward, squatted down low, and prepared to meet the next pitch. *Whack!* He sent the ball flying into the outfield. José and Danny scored easily.

Jumper dropped his glove to the ground. He stood and crossed to the batter's box. Somebody on the Crawford bench groaned.

Jumper removed his baseball cap, wiped sweat from his forehead, and studied the playing field. Then he slapped his cap back on his head, touched the brim for luck, and stepped boldly into the batter's box. He was terrified of striking out. He glared daringly at the pitcher, determined not to let the boy know just how scared he was. There was no time for mistakes. With Marcus on second, he needed to hit at least a single.

Jumper told himself all he had to do was to connect with the ball. He dug the tips of his cleats into the dirt, lifted the bat over his shoulder, and took a couple of practice swings.

"You're the man!" Nico yelled from the Crawfords' bench.

"Hey, Jumper, we're counting on you!" José shouted.

"Come on, Jumper," Dakota called out.

Jumper looked back at the bench and nodded. The pressure had him sweating more than the hot sun. He cocked his bat and stood legs spread wide, body down low. The ball sailed toward him. He took his time and decided not to go for the first pitch.

"Ball one," the umpire called.

Relieved, Jumper resumed his batting stance. He glanced up at first base and caught Nia winking at him.

Jumper turned his attention back to the pitcher. He swung enthusiastically at the next pitch . . . and missed the ball widely.

"Strike one!" the umpire boomed.

Jumper readied himself and tried again.

"Strike two!"

Jumper kicked the dirt angrily. His heart pounded hard against his chest wall. Coach approached him and whispered in his ear that he should bunt.

Jumper nodded. He'd been practicing bunting and

seemed better at it than hitting the ball into the outfield. If he bunted, Marcus would advance to third and he'd be safe at first. It would keep the Crawfords alive.

Jumper knew he was supposed to keep his head down, but he looked up quickly to check Marcus's readiness. Both of them had to run really fast.

Jumper put his head back down and gripped the bat. The tension in his body worked against him. He knew that he was gripping the bat too tightly but he just couldn't relax.

Jumper watched as the pitcher wound up and let the ball rip. He kept his eyes on the ball until it neared his body. Then he eased the barrel of the bat forward, trying to keep it at a forty-five-degree angle like he'd been taught. The aluminum bat stung his hands as it connected with the ball. Instead of bunting down, the ball shot up into the air. Jumper was too stunned to move.

"Run, Jumper. Run!" the entire Crawfords' bench shouted as they jumped to their feet.

Jumper dropped his bat and took off.

The ball flew high into the air. Jumper ran as fast as he could, not looking at anything. He reached first base just as Marcus touched third base and the ball landed smack in the glove of the right fielder.

The victorious Black Stockings rushed their pitcher. The Crawfords stood in stunned silence.

The game was over, but Jumper felt an odd sense of victory. Okay, his team had lost, but Jumper got his first hit during a game; surely that counted for something with his teammates. He strolled back to the bench.

Marcus stepped into his path. His eyes were dark and cold.

Jumper frowned.

"Don't you learn nothing?" Marcus sneered.

"What, you never popped out?" Jumper retorted.

"Coach told you to bunt!"

"Yeah, well, I tried!"

"Yeah . . . well, next time, *stupid*, keep the barrel below your hands!"

Jumper felt crushed. Marcus was right. Still, he was furious at the attack. He brushed past Marcus and bent to retrieve his glove from under the bench.

Marcus put his foot on the glove. Then he stomped the glove into the dirt.

Jumper shoved Marcus and sent him flying backward.

Marcus scrambled to his feet and jumped into

Jumper's face. He pushed him back. "Back off, 'burb, unless you want to meet me later," Marcus warned.

Coach Coleman stepped between them and stood silently.

Jumper froze and let his hands fall to his sides.

Marcus backed up and unclenched his fists.

"Ten laps, both of you! Then report to my office," the coach barked.

Twenty minutes later, the tired and sweaty boys trudged into the coach's office.

"Who wants to begin?" Coach Coleman asked the boys.

"He started it, Coach," Marcus replied.

Jumper jumped up from his seat. "He stepped on my glove," he said.

"Sit down, Jumper," Coach snapped. "I don't care who started what. What I saw was unacceptable. Whatever led up to that little display of temper could have been dealt with another way. We've talked enough about respecting each other — respect doesn't stop after the game. You hear me?"

Heads bobbed.

Jumper listened quietly. He was scared that Coach would ask him to leave camp. At first, he'd have given anything to be kicked out. Now he wanted to stay. He wanted that badly. The camp gave him somewhere to go . . . and something to prove.

"Marcus, do you understand what it means to be the captain?"

"Yes, Coach," he replied.

"Tell me."

"I'm supposed to lead. Keep the team working together," Marcus replied.

"And did you?"

"Not really, Coach," he admitted.

"Got something to say to Jumper?"

"'Suppose . . .'"

"Let's hear it."

Marcus reluctantly turned and faced Jumper. "Sorry," he mumbled.

Jumper nodded toward Marcus. "Me, too," he replied.

"Marcus, you've got the advantage. You know the game and play it well. Plus, you've been a captain." He paused. "I expect more from you. I've also got confidence that Jumper will be successful, but I need you to support each other. Any problem with that?"

Jumper looked at Marcus, then back to Coach.

"No," the boys said at the same time.

"Okay. Marcus, starting next week you're going to work with a cocaptain. I want you in my office each morning to go over the plan for the day. You understand?"

Marcus stared at Coach, but he wasn't in a position to dispute his decision. "Yes, Coach," he replied.

Coach Coleman turned to Jumper. "Jumper, Monday's your day."

Jumper's mouth fell open. "For what, Coach?"

"Starting Monday, you're cocaptain of the Crawfords," he repeated.

"But, but Coach . . ."

"Trust me on this one," Coach said firmly.

"Coach, how can we cocaptain?" Marcus asked. He didn't want Jumper on his team, much less as a cocaptain.

"It takes two wings to fly," Coach said simply.

Both boys looked bewildered.

"We'll only win if you cooperate," he said. "See you Monday, Marcus."

Both boys eased out of their chairs. "Hold up a minute, Jumper," the coach said.

Jumper sat back down wondering what else Coach

had to say to him. He considered Coach's words: *It takes two wings to fly*. Could he really work with Marcus?

Marcus left without so much as a glance in Jumper's direction.

Coach stood and walked around the desk. He sat in the seat that Marcus had just vacated. He looked at Jumper. "You're working hard and making progress, Jumper. But there's something blocking you. Something other than athletic ability keeping you from connecting with the ball. Help me out here, Jumper. What's going on? Tell me a little more. You're not from around here, are you?"

"No," he said. "My mom and I moved from Connecticut in June. We live with my grandmother in her brownstone on 136th Street."

"So, you're new to the area?"

"Yeah. I used to visit my grandmother a lot, but I never lived here."

"How do you like it?"

"I don't."

He laughed. "Big difference from Connecticut," he said.

"I miss my friends, too."

"I'm sure you do. Have you made any here yet?"

"Nia and Dakota," Jumper replied and thought a minute. "Kelvin, sort of," he added.

"The boys are keeping their distance, huh?"

Jumper nodded.

"That'll change. Give it time. They're following Marcus's lead. He's top dog around here."

"I know, Coach."

"You've been through a lot of changes in a short time," Coach said.

"Yes."

Coach looked back down at Jumper's glove. "How tough has it been on you since your dad died?"

Jumper teared up. He looked away. "Tough," he said, blinking back the tears. He lifted his eyes back up and met Coach Coleman's understanding gaze.

"I know how you feel," he said softly.

"Why's that? Did your dad die when you were a kid?"

"No," Coach replied shaking his head. "He just left us."

Jumper fixed his eyes on Coach Coleman. "How'd *you* feel when he left, Coach?"

"Angry," he stated emphatically, then stood. "What was his name?" he asked.

Jumper frowned. "Excuse me, Coach?"

"Your father. What was his name?"

"Elijah J. Breeze," he mumbled.

"Like yours," Coach said looking Jumper in the eyes. "It's a strong name," he continued. "I'm glad your father passed it on to you. I'm here for you, Jumper. No special favors, but my door's always open. Got it?"

Jumper nodded. He wanted to know more about how Coach handled his anger toward his father, but didn't dare ask such a personal question. Jumper felt angry with his dad, too. Then, he felt guilty for feeling angry. He shouldn't blame his father for dying. So, being angry just wasn't right.

Still, when Jumper had heard about his father's sudden death he'd felt deserted. He stared at Coach Coleman: What was it like to have your father walk out on you? Was the hurt any different? Was it more painful to know that your father was alive and living in some other state instead in some unimaginable place called heaven? Was the pain really that much different? Did it matter how you lost your father?

Jumper looked away from Coach Coleman, wondering if his father had left him to live with some other boy.

CHAPTER SEVEN

Jumper woke the next morning still feeling tired. Friday was a party night in Harlem, so the sounds of rap music and laughter from the street had kept him up pretty late. His mom had suggested that he move his room to the back of the house, but Jumper liked watching the action on the block.

Jumper was happy for the weekend break from baseball camp. He stretched and his body screamed with muscle aches from the week's strenuous workouts. Lying on his back, he considered his options. He decided that going to Connecticut was his best bet. Before he moved, he had promised his friends that he'd visit often, but he hadn't seen them since June.

Jumper hopped out of bed, showered, dressed, and

raced downstairs to ask his mother if he could call
Kenny and Chris.

"Good morning, Jumper. You're just in time for waf-
fles," she said in reply. Ever since their talk, things had
been good between them.

"With bacon?" he added, pulling out a stool and
climbing onto it.

"You got it."

Leaning his elbows on the counter, Jumper stared at
his mother through the passageway.

"Did something happen at camp yesterday?"

"Why?" he asked. Had Coach called his mom to tell
her about the fight?

"You seemed in a bad mood last night so I thought
something was wrong."

Oh, he thought. He'd given himself away. Jumper
pretended to busy himself with the syrup bottle. He
moved it around like it was a toy on wheels while
he tried to figure out if he should tell his mother about
Marcus. "Camp was all right," he said, looking up.

His mom lifted slices of bacon. "Still having diffi-
culty hitting?" she asked.

He nodded. *That and a few other things, like the fact that
my team captain hates me, my only real friends at camp are silly*

girls who are more interested in my dimples than me, and I have no idea what to do about my discussion with the coach.

Other than that, camp was going just fine.

"It's amazing how hard it is to hit that little round ball, isn't it?" his mother continued.

"How would you know?" asked Jumper.

"We used to play baseball here in the streets when I was growing up," his mother replied. "Street ball, we called it. I never could hit that ball," she laughed. "But, I didn't take it seriously, either. I wasn't part of a real team. I'm sure being on a team makes a difference. Makes it harder, I guess."

Jumper fought back tears of frustration and anger. He wanted to scream at his mother that hitting the stupid baseball wasn't the issue. Didn't she understand anything?

His mom turned the bacon over and kept chatting. She was in a good mood these days, he thought. "It takes time. I'm sure the coach tells you so."

"I don't have time," he muttered.

Carolyn's head snapped up. "What do you mean?"

"We just finished two weeks of practice and a week of games. Next week we're in the camp play-offs, Mom."

"Yes. So?"

"The winner of the play-offs goes on to represent Harlem in the citywide games. I'm on the team that won last year and I stink." Jumper sighed.

His mother took the bacon out of the pan, opened the waffle iron and took out a steaming-hot waffle, placed both on a plate, and handed it to her son. Next, she pulled up a stool next to him and gave him her full attention. "What else is bothering you, Jumper?" she asked.

Jumper crunched the crisp bacon and poured syrup on his waffle, ignoring her question. He needed a few extra seconds to get his story straight. If it wasn't hitting the ball, what *was* the problem? He gobbled down half the waffle and two slices of bacon before he spoke.

"This kid Marcus and I almost got into it yesterday," he began. "Coach Coleman stepped in and stopped us. Marcus is making my life miserable," Jumper finally admitted. "Even worse, he's the captain of the team."

"Oh," his mom replied. "Tell me about it."

"Marcus bosses everybody. None of the other boys will even talk to me. I mean on the field it's okay but they won't be seen with me off the field. I think it's because they're afraid of making Marcus mad."

"So what happened yesterday? Why did you and Marcus fight?"

"We didn't fight really. Coach stepped between us."

"Okay. Almost fight."

He finished off his waffle, then explained the situation.

"What did the coach do?"

"Made us run laps to cool off, then lectured us. He's making Marcus have cocaptains all next week. It's a blow to Marcus, especially because I'm the first cocaptain. It could cost us as a team."

"Or it could pull the team together and make you more effective."

"That's what Coach says. He said something else that we didn't really understand."

"What was that?"

"It takes two wings to fly," Jumper repeated, looking to his mother for an explanation.

His mother chuckled. "He's a smart guy," she said. "That's a proverb."

"Like birds need two wings? Planes need both wings?"

"Exactly. Coach wants you and Marcus to learn to cooperate. He's taking it a step further by making him work with a cocaptain during play-offs. The stakes are higher, therefore Marcus is forced to work harder as a leader. If it works, the team will be successful."

"I'm not sure if Marcus and I can ever work together," Jumper muttered.

"If you don't, you'll lose, the team will lose, and you'll miss an important learning opportunity, too. You *have* to work together," she said firmly.

Jumper got down from the stool and took his plate to the sink. "Mom, I want to go to Connecticut today."

"Sounds like a plan," his mom replied. "We could stop by and visit some friends and go to lunch at the beach," she offered.

"No, I want to spend the day with Chris and Kenny."

She nodded. "Okay. Call them."

"If they're home, will you drive me there?"

"Sure," Carolyn said.

"Can I spend the night?"

"Of course."

Jumper disappeared into the living room and started dialing. First, he got Kenny's answering machine. Then he got Chris's mother. Chris had stayed on for another session at basketball sleepaway camp. Jumper hung up; he wished he was with Chris right now.

Jumper stretched out on the couch trying to think of an alternate plan. He couldn't take another Saturday at his grandmother's Laundromat. He didn't feel like spending a day in the arcade. He thought about going to the neighborhood recreation center for a swim, but nixed that idea because he didn't want to go alone. He could call Nia or Dakota. No, he wasn't in the mood for their chatter. Instead, he decided to wander the neighborhood, maybe go by the basketball courts and join a pickup game.

By the time Jumper ventured outside it was already hot and humid. Sweat beaded on his forehead. He reached the basketball courts and sat on the edge, watching the boys shoot baskets. Their balls bounced and flew high into the air and swished down through nets. The boys made more baskets than they missed. He wondered how he'd do if he joined them. But he couldn't imagine any further embarrassment. He couldn't risk more rejection. No, these boys were serious about their game. And they were good.

The free shooting stopped. The boys met in the middle

of the court and divided up. Two stood in the middle while the others stepped back. A jump ball would decide which team went first.

Jumper ducked as the game ball flew in his direction but kept his eyes on the two boys who dove for it. He watched them tussle a few inches away. His eyes connected with one of the boys, the one holding on to the ball. Finally, the struggle ended and they got up.

Jumper grinned at the boy with the ball.

The boy stood, brushed off, and approached him.

"You play?"

Jumper nodded.

"Good. We need help."

He rose reluctantly.

"Let's go," the boy urged.

"Okay," he replied.

"Name?"

"Jumper."

"Mike," he replied, knocking knuckles in greeting. "Hey," he yelled to the others. "We got another man. Name's Jumper."

Jumper jumped in and quickly adjusted to the aggressive style of play. He fought, grabbed the ball, rebounded, and shot baskets. In the final quarter, his team pulled into the lead. Mike called them over for a talk. He high-fived Jumper and they went back out determined to maintain their lead. Jumper played like it was the championships. For the first time since the move to Harlem, he was confident.

Mike and the boys beat the other team by two points. They celebrated their big win with some cold sodas.

"We be balling around this time tomorrow," Mike told Jumper before they parted. "Come on by."

"Word," Jumper replied.

He started toward home a new way. It took him into a part of the park that he'd never explored. Why did basketball come so easy when baseball was so hard? Was it the game? Or was it him? He'd always been a good athlete. Soccer had come easy. He was a natural at basketball. But with baseball he was a failure.

Jumper thought about his father. They used to talk about how he seemed to avoid things that were difficult. His father had noticed it when Jumper first took swimming lessons. He had been the only five-year-old who was afraid to jump in the water. He hated getting his face wet.

Jumper told his father that he didn't want to go back to swimming. His father coaxed an explanation out of him; then he came up with a game to help Jumper get comfortable with dunking his face in the water. It worked: Jumper, without his fear, learned to swim.

I really need Dad now, he thought.

Jumper turned down a path and heard noises in the distance. He thought he heard a girl yell. He looked from side to side as he walked; something felt really wrong. Suddenly, he spotted a pile of girls on the ground in front of him. He headed in their direction. They were fighting. He debated about going forward or turning back in the opposite direction.

"Help!" he heard a small voice yell.

Jumper started to run toward the girls. As he neared them, he saw a girl punch and kick a small girl who was pinned to the ground. Jumper didn't stop to think. He rushed in to help the girl on the ground.

"Get off her," Jumper yelled. He yanked the bigger girl off the smaller one. "Nia," he said when he recognized the smaller girl.

The other girls ran off in different directions. They cursed and shouted and promised to finish what they'd started. Jumper counted five girls twice Nia's size. He wondered what this was all about.

Jumper reached down and pulled Nia up. She was

crying. He felt weird. "Don't cry, Nia," he said. It was all he could think of to do. "Are you hurt?"

Nia wrapped her arms around her belly and stood up straight. She looked up at Jumper. "Stupid girls," she said. "They started calling me little and pushing me around."

"You *know* them?"

"Yeah. Well, one anyway. Shanequa, the one that was punching me," she replied. "Come on," Nia said standing up. "Let's walk. I need to get out of here."

"Okay, I'll walk you home."

They started walking and talking.

"Shanequa lives in my building with her aunt. She lied to her. Said she was with me and she wasn't. When her aunt asked me if we'd gone to the movies together, I told her no. Anyway, Shanequa got in trouble. Had to stay in the apartment over the weekend," Nia said. "She was hot."

"So, she and her friends beat you up?"

"Yeah. It's not the first time. They jumped me one time before 'cause I told the manager at our building that they'd stolen some money from a kid on the playground."

"Did you get hurt?"

"No. They got scared off by some kids who came into the lobby."

"Does Marcus know?"

Nia laughed. "He's always arguing with Shanequa's brother."

"Oh, great. One big happy family. And you live in the same building?"

"That's right."

"Do you think she'll come after you again?"

"Who knows? I'm going to stay out of her way," Nia said.

"Sounds like a good idea," he replied.

They turned down 146th Street and stopped in front of a big apartment building on the corner of Convent and 146th.

"Don't mention this to anyone, hear me?" Nia said.

He nodded. "I won't."

She smiled. "You're brave, you know?"

"Not really."

"Yes, you are!" she insisted. "The girls coulda turned on you."

"I didn't even think about that," Jumper said.

"That's 'cause you're too brave."

"So are you, Nia," Jumper said.

"See you in camp," Nia answered.

"Yeah," he said and watched her push through the crowded stairwell. Nia was so tiny and tough. Jumper stuffed his hands in his pockets and pressed on. It'd been a good day so far.

CHAPTER EIGHT

Jumper arrived at camp fresh and determined.

Marcus was waiting for him.

The cocaptains exchanged glances.

Working together was going to be tough.

Jumper stopped at the coach's office and stood stiffly next to Marcus as Coach Coleman gave them their assignment for the day.

"This week we're going to work on team building. The tension between you two is affecting how well your team works. Do you agree?"

Jumper looked down.

Marcus cleared his throat.

Neither boy spoke.

"I'll take that as a yes. Jumper, what is Marcus's strength?"

Jumper looked up, wide-eyed. "His strength?"

"That's right. What's he good at?"

He looked over at the boy who'd harassed him from day one. "He's good at turning a double play," he said.

"Okay. Good point. Marcus, what about Jumper?"

Marcus looked over at Jumper and hesitated. "I don't know him, Coach."

"No, you don't, but I'm sure you've seen something about him that makes him an asset to the team?"

"Well, he misses pop-ups and can't hit the ball," Marcus spat.

"Which obviously makes you mad."

"I want to win, Coach. Is that so wrong?"

"No. I understand your concern, but I expect that you'll come up with a creative way to help Jumper improve his skills. So, I'll ask you again. What about Jumper makes him an asset to the team?"

Marcus shuffled in place. "He works hard," he finally admitted. "I've seen him at the batting cage working on his swing."

"Good answer. I'm proud of both of you," Coach said.

Jumper's shoulders dropped with relief. He had no idea that Marcus paid any attention to him.

"Now, let's take this a step further. Marcus has baseball skills and experience as a team leader. Jumper's newer at the game, but is willing to work hard to gain some skills. He hasn't led a team, yet seems to have leadership qualities: willingness to see positives in others, persistence and determination, team experience from his basketball days. Tell me something, Jumper, who makes you do your homework at night?"

Jumper frowned. "Nobody makes me, Coach. My parents, well, my mom now, she checks my work, but I do it myself."

"You've played on a team before, right?"

"Yes, soccer first, then basketball."

"Good. Were you ever late for practice?"

"My coach wouldn't allow it."

"Do you want to play baseball?"

"I didn't at first, but now I do."

"And, why's that?"

"'Cause I want to prove something, I guess."

"What are you trying to prove?"

"Well, my dad used to warn me that just 'cause something is hard I shouldn't avoid it. He got real mad at me when I quit before. So now even though baseball is hard for me, I don't want to quit."

"What do you have to say now, Marcus?" Coach asked.

"I get your point, Coach."

"Okay. Then, for today you'll take direction from Jumper along with the rest of the team. I want you to spend the morning working with players who need help. Who do you think that is?"

"Aisha, Brooklyn, and Michael mostly."

"What about Jumper?"

"What about him?"

"I want you to spend time with him at the batting cage," Coach Coleman replied.

Marcus looked away.

"Do you understand?"

He looked back up. Anger boiled just below the surface. "Yes, Coach."

"We'll meet with the whole team this afternoon and evaluate the day. Now, get out there and make this a good one."

The team seemed confused by the shift in leadership,

but caught on and responded to Jumper's calm direction. They spent the morning on drills. Midmorning, Jumper and Marcus headed to the batting cage for hitting practice. They stood side by side batting from separate machines.

Neither boy spoke.

When Coach wandered over, he changed that. The boys were forced to work together. While Jumper hit the balls, Marcus begrudgingly advised him on technique and focus. Coach observed and commented when he needed to. He was pleased with both boys. After thirty minutes, he dismissed them for lunch. They separated quickly and headed in different directions.

Jumper sat with Nia and Tony at lunch. Several other kids joined them. Word had spread about the fight in the park. Everybody was curious about the boy who'd pulled Nia from the gang of girls.

Jumper chatted cheerfully; for the first time he felt like part of the group. Still, he worried about the afternoon. Would he embarrass himself during the game?

As Jumper was putting his lunch tray away, Kelvin approached. "Thanks for helping Nia out," he said.

"You would have done the same thing," he responded.

"True. She's like a sister to me," he added. "I hear that you're the captain of the Crawfords today."

"Cocaptain," he reminded Kelvin. "What about you?"

"Coach assigned me to be cocaptain of the Black Stockings, which means we battle each other today," Kelvin said.

"Are you nervous?" Jumper asked.

"Not really. You?"

"Kind of," Jumper answered.

"Well, good luck," Kelvin offered.

"You, too."

"Hey, Jumper," Kelvin called over his shoulder. "Let's hang out after the game."

"Sounds like a plan," Jumper said.

The boys knocked knuckles and went back to their respective teams.

The game was under way.

By the sixth inning, the Black Stockings were ahead by one and there were two outs. Jumper was up. He'd struck out the first time . . . and was plenty worried now. From the corner of his eye, he saw his teammates packing it in. They were gathering their gloves and preparing to go back into the field. It was humiliating.

Jumper bent into batting position, focused, and waited for the first pitch. He swung wildly, missing the ball completely. His teammates grumbled. Jumper readied himself for the next pitch. The ball headed straight for him. He kept his eyes glued to the ball and swung with confidence. *Whack!* Bat and ball connected and Jumper took off. The ball shot through the hole between first and second. By the time the right fielder stopped it, Jumper had already landed safely on first base.

The Crawfords' bench was up and cheering.

Jumper couldn't believe his luck.

The next batter hit a grounder to first which ended the inning. The Crawfords took to the field.

Jumper assumed his position in center field. His team kept the Black Stockings from scoring any more runs in the next three innings, but the Stockings still won the game.

After the game, Jumper and Kelvin shook hands.

"Good game," Jumper said.

"Good hit," Kelvin replied. "How'd you like being cocaptain?"

"I liked it. Think Marcus is mad about the loss?"

"He's always mad. I wouldn't worry 'bout him. He'll get over it. I'll talk to him."

"Thanks."

"So what do you want to do now?"

"I don't know," Jumper replied. "I have to stop at my house first, though. We could go to the park and ball a while."

"You been balling?" Kelvin asked.

Jumper laughed. "Some."

"Let's go. First, we got to stop by Coach's office. Then we can head uptown. You can show me what you know on the courts."

"More than baseball, I can tell you that," Jumper replied.

They started to walk off when Jumper remembered his glove. "Oh, my glove," he said stopping abruptly. He raced over to the bench to retrieve his glove, but it was gone. Jumper walked slowly back toward Kelvin.

"Where's your glove?" Kelvin asked.

"It wasn't where I left it. Think someone took it?"

"Why would they?"

"Don't know — but I've got to find it."

"Get in trouble with moms, huh."

"Well, it's more than that,"

"More than what?"

"It belonged to my dad."

"Oh, so pops will be mad."

Jumper shook his head. "He's dead."

"Oh, sorry, man. Come on . . . let's check in the office. Probably somebody turned it in. You know, they probably picked it up by mistake thinking it was theirs. Yeah, you'll get it back. Don't worry."

"Look, if it's not there don't say anything to Coach," Jumper said.

"Why?" Kelvin asked.

"I don't want to get anyone in trouble. We can figure this out," Jumper replied.

"Word," Kelvin said with growing respect for his new friend. Maybe Marcus was wrong about Jumper. He didn't seem like a nerd. He wasn't a snob. He was okay.

The boys talked all the way to Coach's office.

"My dad lives in St. Croix," Kelvin said.

"Where's that?" Jumper asked.

"In the Virgin Islands."

"Ever been there?"

"Yeah, twice."

"What's it like?"

"Cool. Lots of beaches with water so clear you can see the bottom."

"I love to swim!" Jumper said.

"Me, too," said Kelvin. "And, you can swim in the winter."

"It doesn't get cold down there?" Jumper asked.

"What? It's warm all year-round," Kelvin bragged.

"Word! So, it's just you and your mom?" he asked.

"No, I have a little brother named David and a step-dad. What 'bout you?" Kelvin asked. "Got any brothers and sisters?"

"No, it's just me," answered Jumper. "Since my dad died, I live with my mom and grandmother."

"How'd he die?"

"Heart attack."

"Really! Was he old?" Kelvin asked.

"No, he wasn't," Jumper replied.

"I didn't know someone young could have a heart attack," Kelvin said.

"Yeah, well — I didn't, either, till it happened," said Jumper.

"That's tough. Hope my dad doesn't have a heart attack," Kelvin said aloud.

Jumper wished he could reassure Kelvin, but he had learned that anything was possible.

"Is that why you moved to Harlem?" Kelvin asked.

"Yeah, Mom thought it would be better to live with my grandmother," said Jumper.

"Didn't you want to move?"

"I didn't have a choice," Jumper said.

"It's hard to change schools and get used to a new neighborhood," Kelvin said.

Jumper laughed. "Got that right. You ever move?"

"You kidding? We move all the time. I must have lived in six different apartments so far," Kelvin replied.

The boys walked on in silence. Jumper wondered why Kelvin was willing to be friends now. What had changed?

"Marcus is gonna be really mad 'cause you're talking to me," Jumper said.

Kelvin shrugged. "I don't care."

"Why now?"

"What's that?"

"Why you talking to me now?"

Kelvin looked at Jumper. "I love Nia like a sister. Most of us do. She's little and mouthy but wouldn't hurt nobody. The girls that jumped her have been warned. We don't play that."

"I don't know her like you do, but I feel like that, too."

Kelvin and Jumper crowded into Coach's small office with the rest of the kids. "Jumper and Kelvin, good job today," Coach began. Looking around the group, he added, "You'll all get a chance to lead. Leaders," he reminded them, "have to be able to follow."

The teams talked about how they were feeling as a team and set goals for the next few days. Before dismissing them, Coach praised their efforts. "You're coming together. I like that. Tomorrow, we'll switch things up. Dakota and Nia will be the cocaptains. Thanks, everyone. See you in the morning."

Jumper and Kelvin pulled Nia and Dakota aside. They wanted the girls to succeed so they offered them some advice. Then Kelvin let them in on the search for the stolen glove.

"Jumper's glove was taken," Kelvin began.

"Someone stole your glove?" Nia jumped to his defense.

"I don't know, Nia. It's just missing. Could've been a mistake."

"Not likely," she said.

"Are you and Marcus fighting?" Dakota asked.

"Not really," Jumper said.

"Yes, you are," Nia stated. "I live with that boy! He's

always complaining about you, so it wouldn't surprise me if he took your glove!"

"Nia, we don't know *who* took Jumper's glove," Kelvin reminded her.

"Better tell Coach," Nia said. "He'll get to the bottom of this!"

"I don't want to rat on anybody," Jumper insisted. "I just want my glove back."

"Look, Nia and Dakota, you both hear things. Someone will be talking. So just keep your eyes and ears open and tell Jumper or me if you hear anything. We'll take it from there," Kelvin instructed.

They agreed to the plan, then walked across town and took the subway. When they reached their stop, they parted ways. The girls headed uptown. The boys walked over to Jumper's house.

"You think Nia's right? Should I tell Coach about my missing glove?" Jumper asked Kelvin as they walked up his stoop.

"Possibly, but give me till tomorrow to find out if Marcus took it. If he did, I'll know soon," Kelvin answered.

"Okay. Just don't mention the lost glove to my mom. She doesn't need to know," Jumper told him as they reached the front door. He opened it and shouted to his mom.

"Jumper, I'm upstairs. Come on up," she replied.

"Kelvin's with me."

"Bring him up, too," she called back down.

The boys took the steps two at a time. They dropped their bags off on Jumper's floor and climbed the last flight of steps to his mom's floor. They found her painting in the back room.

"Mom, this is Kelvin," Jumper introduced his friend.

His mom put down her paintbrush and smiled at Kelvin. "I'm glad you came over," she said, offering him her hand.

"Me, too," Kelvin replied. His eyes quickly shifted to the painting. It was a neighborhood scene. "That's the Abyssinian Baptist Church, right?" He asked, pointing to the white-stone building with a steeple and folks dressed to the nines, spilling out onto the sidewalk.

"I call it *Sunday Morning*," Jumper's mom said, smiling. "Do you paint?"

"Well . . ." Kelvin said hesitantly. "I draw with colored pens mostly."

"You like art, then?" she asked.

"Yeah," he admitted.

"Have you taken art classes?" she asked.

"My school doesn't have art class," Kelvin replied.

"Oh, that's too bad."

"Jumper told me about your new job," he said.

"Yes. I'm excited. It's a good school with both art and music departments. Maybe you'll come there for high school."

"Maybe," Kelvin said.

"I'm hungry, Mom," Jumper interrupted.

"Go down to the kitchen. Your grandmother fried some chicken before she left for work. It's on the stove. There's juice in the refrigerator."

Jumper grabbed Kelvin's sleeve. "Let's go, man."

Kelvin held back. "Um, Mrs. Breeze, think you can teach me how to paint?" he asked.

She nodded. "After you've had something to eat, come on back up. I'll set you and Jumper up with a clean paper."

"Word!" Kelvin replied. "I mean . . . thanks," he corrected himself.

Jumper's mom laughed. "You're welcome."

The boys raced down the stairs, jumping off the last step onto the landing with a bang. "You really want to paint?" Jumper asked as they tore into the warm spicy chicken.

"Don't tell the others," Kelvin said. He held a chicken leg to his lips and took a big bite. "I think I could be good at it," he added. "Are you any good?"

"Painting's my mom's thing. I don't do it much," Jumper said.

"Is it okay if we try it today?"

"Of course," Jumper replied.

They ate quickly, swallowed a glass of juice, then walked back upstairs to try their hands with the paintbrush.

Jumper's mother was setting up the tripods and singing along with Luther Vandross when they reached upstairs. Over the next two hours, Mrs. Breeze taught the boys the basics of watercolors.

"Think you're going to like teaching, Mom?" Jumper asked as he started his painting.

"I think so, Jumper. I won't know for sure until school begins, but I like a number of the other teachers. There's an excitement to new beginnings, don't you think?"

"Yes and no."

"You're going to PS 42, aren't you?" Kelvin asked Jumper as he began to mix bluish-green paint.

"Why, do you go there, too?" Jumper asked.

"No. But I hear it's nice. Better than my school," Kelvin replied.

"All I know is that if I can make it with the Crawfords, I can make it anywhere," Jumper joked.

"Nia and Dakota go there, you know?"

Jumper looked up from his art. "They told me. What about Marcus?"

"Marcus goes to St. Catherine's."

"How come?"

"'Cause he kept getting in trouble in public school so his mother tried something else," Kelvin said.

"Speaking of new situations, how did you like being cocaptain of the Crawfords, Jumper?" his mom asked.

"It was okay," he said. "Kelvin was captain of the Black Stockings."

"Did your teammates listen to you?" she asked.

"Yes. Coach was right there helping us make decisions," Jumper told her. "We lost," he added.

"But Jumper did a good job," Kelvin confirmed. "And he played better, too!"

"That's good news. Did you get a hit?"

"I singled and struck out," he answered. His missing glove was on his mind. He felt guilty not telling his mother about it.

"That's good, Jumper!" she praised. "How did Marcus handle the loss?"

"He gave me a look," Jumper said and thought again about his glove.

"With Coach breathing down his neck, Marcus had to act cool but you could tell he was steaming," Kelvin said.

"Did Coach assign cocaptains for tomorrow's game?"

"Nia and Dakota," Jumper replied. "We gave them some pointers."

"I'm sure you did," Mrs. Breeze said. She studied Kelvin's paper. "Sunrise?"

Kelvin shook his head. "Sunset over the ocean. It's how I remember my last trip to St. Croix."

"Kelvin's dad lives in the Virgin Islands," Jumper told his mom.

"Have you been there?" Kelvin asked Mrs. Breeze.

"Jumper's dad and I went to St. Thomas once. We took a ferry over to St. John, but didn't make it to St. Croix. Is it nice?" she asked.

"Yeah. I haven't been in a while," Kelvin told her.

"What else will you put in your picture besides the ocean and the setting sun?" Mrs. Breeze asked.

"A fisherman, like my dad," he replied. "My father likes to go fishing early in the morning or at sunset. When I visited him, I spent a lot of time watching sunsets," he answered.

"What color is his boat?" Jumper's mom asked.

Kelvin smiled and dipped his paintbrush into the red paint. "Red," he said and began painting a boat.

"Is the ocean really that color?" Jumper asked, looking over at Kelvin's painting.

"Yeah. It goes from pale green to dark blue as it gets deeper," he answered. "That's the colors of the Caribbean. The water's warm and clear. You can see the bottom."

"Not like the cold, brown Atlantic," Jumper added.

"You paint a lovely picture, Kelvin," Jumper's mother said. She smiled at her son's new friend. "Do you get to see much of your dad?"

"Not really," Kelvin answered. "I've gone to St. Croix twice, but my dad comes to New York every few years."

"Mom, have I ever been to the Virgin Islands?" Jumper asked.

"No, but we took you to Jamaica once. You may not remember it, though. You were three."

"Can we go to St. Croix?" he asked.

"Maybe," his mom replied.

"When?" Jumper persisted.

"I don't know, Jumper," she said, looking at his canvas. "That looks like our brownstone."

"It is."

"What else will you put in the picture?"

He looked up at his mom. "A boy."

She winked at her son. "What will you call your picture?"

"*Home*," Jumper said.

CHAPTER NINE

"Manhunt?"

"That's right."

"How's it played?"

"Two hide; two find. When you're captured, the team has to say 'manhunt one-two-three' three times," Kelvin explained.

Jumper nodded. "Sounds like hide-and-seek to me," he said.

"Ghetto style," Kelvin replied, laughing. "We'll be hiding in the projects. Right here in Building 400."

Jumper was spending the afternoon at Kelvin's apartment. Danny and Francisco, two boys from camp, were over, too. The four boys were sitting in Kelvin's living room trying to come up with an alternate activity.

They'd planned to play basketball, but thunderstorms forced them inside.

Jumper didn't answer right away. He wasn't sure he wanted to play hide-and-seek in a twenty-five-story apartment building.

Danny sensing his concern jumped in. "Jumper won't know his way around. He should stay with you, Kelvin. You hide. Francisco and I will find you."

"Yeah," said Francisco. "Kelvin has walkie-talkies just in case you get separated. It'll be fun."

"Okay," Jumper agreed.

The boys stood and prepared to head out on an adventure. Kelvin let his mom know their plans and got the walkie-talkies from his room.

"Rules," Kelvin said when he returned to the living room.

"We stay in Building 400," Danny started.

"Rooftop's off-limits," Francisco added.

"Right. No rooftop — it's too dangerous," Kelvin agreed. "Come on, Jumper. Give us five minutes, then come find us." In the hallway, Kelvin whispered, "We're going to the basement."

They took the steps. At the bottom, they ran around looking for a hiding space. In the laundry room they hid behind the washing machines. Huddled in the corner, the boys talked softly.

"Can't believe camp's almost over," Jumper said.

"Me, either," Kelvin replied.

"How do our teams stack up compared to last year?"

"We're working harder than last year," Kelvin said. "I like the way Coach gave everybody a chance to be captain."

"Wasn't Nia a surprise!" said Jumper.

"Told you she was mouthy. I'm just glad her mouth got used for something good," Kelvin laughed.

"Marcus still doesn't talk to me," Jumper said.

"He's so stubborn."

"What's that about?"

"Not sure I should be telling you this, but you know about his dad, right?"

"No."

"Well, his dad's in a wheelchair," Kelvin said slowly. "He drinks a lot and is real mean to Marcus."

"Really?"

"Yeah. His mom fights with his dad and with Marcus and his brothers. Everybody just ignores Nia. Sometimes I hate to go over to their place. Someone's always yelling or throwing things."

"That's too bad, but what's it got to do with me?"

"Marcus thinks you're from a nice family. He was surprised when I told him that your dad died recently."

"You talked to him about me?" asked Jumper.

Kelvin nodded. "Sorry."

Jumper shrugged. "It's okay. Did Marcus say anything to you about my glove?"

"Huh . . . I've been meaning to talk to you about that," Kelvin began.

Jumper felt like screaming but kept his voice down because they were hiding. "He took it, didn't he?!"

"I think so, Jumper. Marcus didn't exactly say that, but I think he knows where it is."

"I can't sit here," Jumper snapped. He was too mad to sit crouched behind washing machines.

"Where you want to go?"

"I don't care . . . let's just move."

"Okay."

Kelvin lifted his walkie-talkie to his mouth. "Hey, Danny. Francisco."

"Yo, Kelvin. We hear you loud and clear," Danny replied.

"Game's over. We've got some unexpected business," Kelvin said.

"Okay, man. See you tomorrow."

"Over and out," Kelvin said as he led Jumper to the exit.

Jumper decided to walk home. The rain had stopped. He debated with himself all the way home but arrived in his neighborhood without a solution. He wandered into his grandmother's Laundromat and plopped down on a stool in her office.

"What's up?" Miss BB asked.

"Got a problem," Jumper admitted.

"Can I help?" she asked.

Jumper looked at his grandmother. He choked back anger and grief. He still had so many mixed-up bad feelings. It made him think that he'd always be sad.

"Kelvin told me that Marcus knows where my glove is, you know, Dad's glove," Jumper said. "He didn't exactly say it, but I think Marcus took my glove. Grandma, I want to hurt that boy!" he admitted.

"I'm sure you do, but there's got to be another way," Miss BB said calmly. "Do you have any ideas?"

"Honestly, I don't. I've been thinking about it over and over. It's driving me crazy." Jumper sank his head in his hands.

"I suppose you've just answered your question."

"What?" he said looking up.

"Honesty. It's time for honesty."

Jumper stared at his grandmother, then nodded. "I got you, thanks."

He walked out of the Laundromat, his mind steady on his problem with Marcus. His grandmother was right. It was *his* problem and needed to be dealt with honestly.

Jumper tossed and turned most of the night, waiting for morning. He didn't want the confrontation to happen at camp. He would suggest to Marcus that they meet away from camp, just the two of them. But if that didn't work, he was prepared to deal right there at camp and accept whatever punishment came with the confrontation.

Jumper had never had a physical fight, but that didn't matter. He would go toe-to-toe as long as it didn't involve weapons. Stealing was wrong . . . and he wanted his glove back!

Jumper arrived at camp early and waited in the front yard. He spotted Marcus walking with Nico. Jumper crossed the yard and blocked Marcus's path. They were off the camp's grounds. Fair territory.

"What's your problem?" Marcus challenged.

"You're my problem," Jumper retorted.

Marcus laughed. "I can't help you play ball, man."

"I don't need your help. I need my glove back," Jumper said standing firm.

"Your glove?" Marcus asked.

"That's right," said Jumper. "You took my glove and I want it back today!"

"What makes you think I have anything to do with *your* glove?" Marcus sneered.

"I've got my sources," Jumper replied.

"Who? Nia? Kelvin?"

"Doesn't matter — I know it's you and I'm tired of playing games with you, Marcus. I want my glove now!"

"Look, I haven't got time for this. I've got a game this morning." Marcus turned away.

Jumper took a step closer. "You won't be able to play if you don't come clean."

"You threatening me, Jumper Breeze?"

"You better believe it, Marcus Johnson."

The boys faced off. Eyes intent. Hands fisted. Hearts racing. Neither boy noticed that Nico had run off for help until they heard voices shouting at them. Jumper recognized Kelvin and Nia's voices, but he refused to back off.

"Jumper, Marcus," Kelvin shouted. "Marcus, give up the glove."

"Yeah," yelled Nia.

"I don't have any glove!" Marcus protested.

"Yes, you do. Now give it up!" Nia insisted.

A small group surrounded them.

Jumper and Marcus stood in the middle, glaring at one another.

One of the kids looked around and hissed: "Coach Coleman is on his way over here. Get it together."

"We can't afford to sit out a game 'cause you two are feuding!" José said.

"Yeah . . . get it together," a kid named Eddie shouted.

"Quick," yelled another voice.

Marcus took a step backward.

Jumper released a deep sigh.

"Marcus, Jumper — what's going on?" the coach asked as he broke through the circle of kids and entered the center. "It seems you two didn't learn anything!"

"Yes we did, Coach," Jumper said.

"That's right," Marcus added quickly.

"So, what's the tension about?" Coach asked.

"Well, well . . . we were just discussing the lineup for

today's game. We all know how important it is," Jumper replied.

"That's right. I was asking Jumper's advice," Marcus confirmed.

"And Marcus was also telling me how he found my glove," Jumper added. He glared at Marcus. "Isn't that right?"

Marcus nodded. "Yeah, Nico and I found it last night when we were going through all the equipment. We put it away. It's in a locker."

"Okay. Well, let's get going. Warm-ups in five," Coach Coleman said before retreating.

Marcus and Jumper eyed each other. The others turned and followed the coach toward the field.

"Got anything else to say?" Jumper asked Marcus.

"I'll get your glove and bring it to the field," he muttered.

"Sounds good," Jumper replied.

"It's an old, beat-up glove anyway," Marcus spat.

Jumper smiled. "Yeah, but it was my dad's," he said, then walked off.

CHAPTER TEN

The tension between Jumper and Marcus fired up the Crawfords. They won the afternoon's game. Now the series with the Black Stockings was tied. All the Crawfords had to worry about was the final game. It would determine who would represent Harlem at the citywide games.

Coach Coleman scheduled the game for Monday evening. He invited all the campers' families to the last game, promising pizza and sodas for all. Jumper's mom offered to bake brownies. Miss BB planned on frying up a ton of chicken. Other parents and relatives were bringing food, too. The big game was just a few days off.

Sunday morning, Jumper met Nia, Dakota, Kelvin,

and Sabrina. The front wheels of their bikes formed a five-pointed star.

"Let's make an agreement," Nia began.

"What's that?" Sabrina asked.

The others leaned in to hear Nia's suggestion.

"We ride bikes, maybe play some basketball, but no one's allowed to mention the big game," Nia suggested.

"Why?" Jumper asked. He had a million questions. He wanted to know what was at stake. Just what was the big deal about the citywides?

"'Cause we need a break!" Dakota said.

"I agree," added Sabrina.

Kelvin looked over at Jumper. "Okay with you, man?"

Jumper shrugged. He was outnumbered. "Suppose," he said.

"Okay," Nia continued. "Let's ride down to Central Park."

"Sounds good. The park will be mad packed though. You know how it gets on Sundays," Sabrina reminded her.

"That's all right. It'll be fun," Dakota said. "Plus, since the park will be closed to cars, we won't have to worry about them," she added.

The girls shoved off. Kelvin and Jumper rolled in

behind them. On the way to the park, they rode alongside cars, crisscrossed onto sidewalks when traffic got backed up, raced down ramps, then eased their bikes into the park traffic. It was a different kind of packed. There were bikers, joggers, strollers, and roller skaters by the hundreds. It was a beautiful sunny day.

Hot and sweaty, the group stopped along the side of the bike path for ice cream and sodas. The girls left their bikes with Kelvin and Jumper and ran off to watch a mime show on the grass.

"My dad finally called," Kelvin said as soon as they were alone.

"Really?" Jumper answered in surprise. Kelvin had been complaining about his dad because he rarely called him.

"I was mad at first and didn't want to talk with him, but gave in when he invited me down to St. Croix for the Christmas holidays," Kelvin told him.

"Wow! Now, we've got to convince my mom in taking me, too," Jumper said.

"Think she'll agree?" Kelvin asked.

"Don't know."

"Well, if she doesn't want to go, you could come with me," Kelvin suggested.

"Leave my mother on Christmas?"

"I'll be leaving my mother, too," Kelvin reminded him.

"Yeah. But it's different with you," Jumper said.

"How?"

"Well, for one, your mother has a husband and your little brother so she won't be alone," Jumper said.

"Your mother has her mother, don't forget."

"But . . ." he hesitated. "But my mother will be sad this Christmas," Jumper reminded him.

Kelvin gave his comment some thought. "You mean because of your dad?"

Jumper nodded.

"I guess you're right. Well, try to talk her into a vacation on St. Croix. Dad said the festival village opens just after Christmas. They'll be a big parade where people dress all up in costumes and dance down the middle of the street. It's fun! Do you like calypso music?"

"I'm not sure," Jumper replied.

"Steel bands?"

Jumper shrugged.

"Anyway, you'll like it," Kelvin said. "We can fly down together."

"Okay. I'll talk with my mom."

"It'll be hot on St. Croix and probably snowing here," Kelvin added, hoping to sweeten the pot.

"They don't have winter?"

"No. Kids wear shorts all year-round."

"I'm going," Jumper said cheerfully.

Jumper and Kelvin watched the mime show from a distance, both trying hard not to talk about baseball . . . and fathers.

"You worried 'bout tomorrow?" Kelvin finally asked.

Jumper turned to his friend. "Thought we weren't gonna talk about tomorrow?"

"I know, but that's stupid when we're both thinking about it."

"Guess it is kind of stupid," Jumper admitted. He wanted to tell his friend that he was more worried about Marcus blaming him if the Crawfords lost than he was about losing.

"I want the Black Stockings to win, but then I don't care. Coach will put me on the team for the city championship, anyway. He always takes his most seasoned players as backup."

"Oh, I didn't know that, but it makes sense. I wonder if he will play me?"

"You mean if you win?"

"Yeah."

"You know he will. That's what the citywide games are all about, right?"

"I know, but what if I mess up?"

"You won't," Kelvin assured him. "You're good, Jumper, and don't let Marcus make you think differently."

"Thanks, man. Hey, want to take our bikes back to my house, then go practice some baseball?"

"Can't," Kelvin replied. "I've got to get home. I promised my mom that I'd take my brother to the playground."

His comment made Jumper wish he had a brother. "Let's get the girls and get out of here," he said.

The friends parted at the edge of the park.

CHAPTER ELEVEN

Monday evening, Jumper stepped into the batter's box. He swung the bat back and forth in preparation for his first swing. It was only the second inning, but Malcolm, the Black Stockings' pitcher, was already off. He was throwing wildly and had walked Dakota and Danny. With runners on first and second, Jumper considered his options. Given how badly Malcolm was pitching, he debated whether he should swing at the first pitch.

He looked back toward Coach Coleman, then into the stands. Jumper spotted his mother and grandmother. He was glad that they'd made it to his last game, but their presence also added to the pressure. This was the first time they would see him play.

Jumper squinted, trying to make out what Miss BB was yelling to him. He gave up and settled on his mom's easy smile instead. Calm, he turned back to face the pitcher.

Jumper readied his body for the first pitch, not sure how he would react. As he watched the ball speed toward him, he decided not to swing.

"Strike one!" the umpire shouted.

Unnerved, Jumper stepped back into position. His eyes stayed glued to the next ball. It sailed past him. He didn't swing.

"Ball one!"

The next two pitches were balls as well. Jumper waited Malcolm out, sensing that he still didn't have his pitching together. Neither team had scored. If Jumper walked, the bases would be loaded for Marcus and the Crawfords would be in a good position to take the lead.

"Ball four! Take the base," the umpire instructed.

Jumper tossed his bat, removed his helmet, and trotted off to first base while Dakota and Danny advanced to second and third. Just as Jumper hoped: The bases were loaded. He'd made the right decision!

Marcus strode to the plate, swung at the first inside

pitch, and crushed the ball into center field. Dakota and Danny scored. The Crawfords were up by two.

Aisha wasn't so lucky. She struck out after swinging at everything that came her way. Michael popped out, followed by José hitting into the infield; Jumper got tagged out at third.

Over the next two innings, the Crawfords made several critical defensive errors that allowed in runs. The Black Stockings finished the inning by taking over the lead. The score was three to two. Neither team scored in the fifth or the sixth innings. After the seventh inning, Coach Coleman called time-out. The teams gathered in their corners to strategize and get a pep talk from each team captain.

Marcus shouted orders at his teammates. They weren't playing their best, that was for sure.

"We're off today," Marcus began. "We're not working together. We could blow this game or we could take control. What's it gonna be?"

"Take control!" José called out.

"Yeah! Control," Dakota chimed in, the others picked up the chant.

Marcus looked directly at Jumper with questioning eyes.

"Let's do it," said Jumper.

"Okay," Marcus said firmly. "Then, we've got to turn this game around in the eighth and keep our lead through the ninth. Everybody on board?"

Heads nodded.

"Any suggestions?" Marcus asked his teammates.

"Well, we need to be more aggressive," Jumper suggested. "Outfielders need to charge the ball."

"Yeah, runners need to remember to run through the bases," Danny said.

"And, you know how Coach is always telling us that, when we bat, remember to keep our heads down and follow the ball all the way to the catcher's mitt if we don't swing at it," Dakota added.

"Good points," Marcus said. "Now, Malcolm's been off. He'll be replaced by Francisco. Expect that Francisco will pitch more into the strike zone than throw balls. Wait. Don't rush the ball. Give it a chance to reach you so you can judge it better. Got it?"

"Got it!" the team cheered. "Time to play ball!" The Crawfords lined up. Marcus passed each of his teammates, slapping open palms. The team locked arms and shouted, "Win!" before returning to the field.

Jumper glanced over at the stands, but saw that his mother and grandmother were now standing by the fence next to Dakota's mom.

The Black Stockings were up.

Dakota wound up, lifting her right leg above her waist, and sent a fastball straight over the plate!

The batter swung and missed. His body spun around with the extreme effort.

Dakota sent two more strikes that nearly grazed the batter's elbow.

"Strike three!" the umpire yelled, the batter dropped his bat and walked, head down, toward the bench.

The next batter waited out the first two pitches and swung at the third strike. He followed his teammate to the bench.

With two outs, Dakota readied for her third victim. It took only three pitches to bring the Crawfords rushing in from the field, eager to take the lead.

Just as Marcus had predicted, Francisco replaced Malcolm on the pitching mound for the Black Stockings. José was up for the Crawfords, but soon he was behind 0-2 . . . until he belted the third pitch into right field. José was safe at first.

Danny, next up, grounded up the middle. He charged first base, landing safely as José tagged second. Aisha, the next batter, struck out. Then Francisco caught Michael's bunt, but not before José and Danny advanced.

Now there were two outs and players on second and third. Jumper stepped up to the plate. He was sweating profusely.

Jumper gave the pitcher his full attention. He bent his knees and lifted his bat above his shoulders. He nodded toward Francisco.

Francisco fired the ball.

Jumper hesitated.

The ball swished past him just below the waist.

"Strike one!" the umpire yelled.

Jumper shifted nervously. He dug the toe of his cleats into the dirt and wiggled into place. He dipped down into position, raised his bat, and readied for the second pitch.

Francisco sent him another pitch right down the strike zone.

Jumper waited until the ball neared his body, then sliced it down the first baseline and took off running at full speed.

Sabrina bent down and positioned her glove against the dirt. The ball ricocheted off her glove.

Kelvin raced in from right field, scooped the ball up, and fired it to home plate.

The catcher jumped up to catch the ball just as Danny slid into home plate.

"Safe!" shouted the umpire.

The Crawfords cleared the bench and rushed over to congratulate José and Danny. They both turned and gave the thumbs-up to Jumper.

Jumper nodded back.

Marcus was up next. Jumper took a two-step lead off first base, bent down low, and prepared to run the minute Marcus hit the ball. He watched as Marcus lifted the bat high over his right shoulder and squared it behind his back. His body was turned at a right angle to the pitcher. His right foot led.

Marcus leaned in to slam the first pitch, but overshot and missed the ball.

"Strike one!"

He readied for the next pitch, but didn't swing.

"Strike two!"

Jumper shifted on the balls of his feet. He side-stepped and retagged first base.

Marcus scowled at Francisco. He took a few practice swings and settled back into position.

Francisco sent a pitch straight down the middle.

Marcus released his swing while following the pitch until it was within reach then he swung. His body twirled around like a top.

"Strike three! You're out!"

Marcus cursed under his breath. He threw the bat down and stalked off, fuming.

The Crawfords took to the field for the top of the ninth, anxious to keep their slim lead. Anything was possible. The Black Stockings could tie up the game and send it into extra innings. Or they could overpower the Crawfords and regain the lead.

Marcus looked around from his position as shortstop. His eyes locked with Jumper. "I got your back, brother," Jumper yelled from center field.

Marcus nodded toward his teammate. They had no choice. He and Jumper had to work together.

Dakota warmed up her arm, then stood still with the ball clenched between her gloved hand and her chest. She nodded toward the catcher when he signaled, in a series of hand motions, her first pitch.

Eddie strutted confidently into the batter's box, eager to help the Black Stockings tie the game.

Dakota wound up, then fired off a curveball below the strike zone.

"Ball one!"

Dakota caught the return ball thrown by the catcher and readied for her next pitch. But she continued to throw balls.

Eddie walked on base.

Nia followed Eddie. A line drive put Eddie safely on second. Nia was called out at first. Dakota struck Sabrina out, one, two, three.

The Crawfords were only one out away from a win.

Dakota now faced the Black Stockings' pitcher. She wound up, pitched . . . and Francisco singled, sending Eddie to third!

With runners on first and third, Kelvin stepped into the batter's box. The infield moved back, and the outfield prepared for a long one: Kelvin was a power hitter. He swung the bat back and forth, then bent into position.

Dakota sent a pitch straight down the middle, but Kelvin let it go.

Kelvin readied for the second pitch while the runners eased off their bases. They were ready.

Dakota was kept on edge by Francisco who kept threatening to steal a base. Francisco took off. Dakota threw to second hoping to catch him, Francisco dove into the plate headfirst.

Safe!

Unnerved, Dakota wound up and sent the ball flying to Kelvin.

"Ball one," the umpire yelled.

Kelvin pulled his bat up and steadied for the next pitch. He swung full as it sped toward his middle. As the ball and bat connected, Kelvin took off running.

Jumper charged Kelvin's fly ball.

Marcus danced backward. His neck craned as the ball fell from the sky.

The runner at third crossed home plate as the runner at second rounded third on his way home.

Jumper and Marcus had their gloves poised for the catch.

Jumper had a split second to decide. He could shout to Marcus, calling him off the play so that he could catch the ball, or he could slow his charge and let

Marcus catch the ball. The words "I got it!" were on the tip of Jumper's tongue. He froze in place. He watched as Marcus got right under the ball. It fell into his glove. The game was over!

The Crawfords raced into center field jumping up and down and screaming. They knocked Marcus down with the force of their celebration. In the stands, Miss BB was on her feet, yelling. Carolyn jumped up next to her, screaming Jumper's name. Kelvin grabbed Nia's hand and pulled her to center field.

Jumper stood on the fringes unsure of how he should act. Nia jumped on his back and Kelvin grabbed him from the front.

"You're smooth," Kelvin congratulated his friend.

Nia fell off Jumper and tumbled to the ground. She got up and yanked Kelvin away from Jumper as Marcus rose from the circle of teammates.

Marcus looked around for Jumper.

The others backed off as Marcus walked slowly toward Jumper.

They faced off.

"Nice play," Jumper offered.

"You could've gotten it," Marcus said.

"I told you that I had your back," Jumper replied. "Let's go get that pizza and talk about how we're gonna play the championship game."

"Word," said Marcus.

The boys knocked knuckles, and the Crawfords headed off the field.

ACKNOWLEDGMENTS

I have many people to thank for their encouragement, direction, and support with the writing of *Safe at Home*: my editor, Sheila Keenan; Dick Robinson; Barbara Marcus; Jean Feiwel; Lisa Holton; Charisse Meloto; Kristina Albertson; Kadir Nelson; my son and inspiration, Jesse Robinson Simms; the boys and girls at the Harlem RBI program, executive director, Rich Berlin, and baseball and softball coach, Vince Coleman.

Harlem RBI (Reviving Baseball in Inner Cities) is a unique year-round youth development program located in East Harlem, New York. Harlem RBI is designed to promote inner-city youths' interest in baseball, increase their self-esteem, and encourage kids to stay in school. RBI programs, like the one in Harlem, are managed by Major League Baseball in partnership with Boys & Girls Clubs of America. More than 200 programs have been started worldwide reaching nearly 100,000 kids annually.

While working for the Commissioner of Baseball, I came to know the children at Harlem RBI. When I began developing *Safe at Home*, Rich Berlin, Vince

Coleman, and the teachers in REAL Kids (Reading and Enrichment Academy for Learning), a summer program at Harlem RBI, helped me run a series of focus groups. It was a wonderful experience and I learned so much from the kids. I hope they enjoy seeing their hard work reflected in the pages of *Safe at Home*!

Sharon Robinson is an educational consultant for Major League Baseball. She has written several nonfiction books about her father, baseball legend Jackie Robinson.

Prior to joining Major League Baseball, Ms. Robinson had a 20-year career as a nurse-midwife and educator. She has taught at Yale, Columbia, Howard, and Georgetown universities. She has also served as director of the PUSH for Excellence Program and as a fundraiser for The United Negro College Fund and A Better Chance.

This is her first novel for young people. She lives in New York City.

OTHER BOOKS BY
SHARON ROBINSON

Jackie's Nine: Jackie Robinson's Values to Live By

Promises to Keep:
How Jackie Robinson Changed America

Stealing Home